Winter's Blush

The Fantasy Maker Series

Cricket Rohman

Copyright © 2017 by Cricket Rohman

Cover Design by Sweet 'N Spicy Designs

ISBN: 978-0-9994819-3-6

Ebook ISBN: 978-0-9994819-2-9

The book Winter's Blush is dedicated to:
The real Lucky dog and the Malin family that rescued
him.

Acknowledgments

Each person named below contributed to the creation or completion of this novel—from offering encouragement and inspiration to supplying feedback and editing.

My heartfelt gratitude goes out to: Bonny Milne, Jerry Gallegos, the horses, and my horse and dog owning friends in Southern Arizona and Southwest Colorado.

Chapter One

December 13

W inn Wahlberg sat alone at a corner table in the hotel's lounge, feeling like a runaway. Her heart fluttered, and a shiver rushed up her spine. Had she made a huge mistake? Tugging and twisting the strawberry-blond hair at the end of her long ponytail gave her no comfort tonight. What was a twenty-year-old female who'd never left Yuma, Arizona, doing in a fancy, downtown Denver hotel? She sipped her soda and waited for the complete stranger to arrive.

Recalling the minimal amount of information she'd been given about this adventure, she knew she was taking a chance, but nothing felt risky until now. Looking around the room, she saw a few couples holding hands—likely fathers with their grown daughters—and several men at the bar, but no other women by themselves. Winn's wild imagination produced both excitement and hesitation.

Her escort could be a man close to her age, but what if he was much older? Would he be handsome or hard to look at? Highly intelligent or awkwardly average? That is when it dawned on her that the escort might not be a man. Certainly, a woman was capable of showing her around the city and taking her to see some real snow. Would she prefer that arrangement? Winn assumed her escort would be a man but . . . What had she gotten herself into?

I should have asked more questions before leaving Yuma.

Restless, she needed to do something more than fooling with her ponytail. For the tenth time, she checked the contents of her purse. Everything was still there: the keycard to her suite, $300 cash, an itinerary, and a ticket for the flight taking her home in a few days. All provided by The Fantasy Maker.

The itinerary was puzzling, though. There were no entries between meeting her escort and the flight back to Yuma. No events, no locations, nothing. Should she be concerned?

No! I must be in for a bunch of wonderful surprises! The rendezvous with her escort was to take place at seven this evening. Glancing at her watch, the escort was forty-five minutes late. Nervous, Winn resumed her ponytail tugging. She'd suffered her share of rejection during her brief life but never so far from home. She considered going up to her room. If the escort failed to show, she'd spend a day or two looking around Denver by herself, and then fly home.

"May I join you?"

Winn turned toward the smooth, deep voice to see a handsome man standing near her table. Slightly older than she anticipated, he was a looker and likely capable of increasing any woman's heart rate. She hoped he would be a friendly companion and tour guide as he helped her live out her fantasy vacation. She'd wanted to experience city life, a far cry from the dry desert life she'd always known—her Yuma life. And, for the first time ever, see snowflakes fluttering down from the sky.

"Yes, of course. That's the plan, isn't it?" She smiled, hoping her nervousness wasn't too obvious.

"Looks like your drink is a rum and coke." He snapped his fingers to summon the server. "I'll take a scotch and bring another rum and coke for the lady."

Winn quickly added, "Minus the rum, please."

He reached over and stroked her cheek with the back of his hand. "Where've you been all my life, gorgeous?" He gazed at her face as if she were the only woman in the world. "Your eyes sparkle like newly polished jade."

Speechless, not comfortable with flattering compliments, she sipped the last inch of soda from her glass as the man pushed his chair back and stood up.

"I shall return. Don't go anywhere, beautiful lady."

Her leg swung up and down under the table. *I am excited, not uneasy.* She said those words many times, hoping her lie might become the truth. Determined, she vowed to enjoy every second of this five-day fantasy vacation she'd been awarded.

He returned, carrying his scotch and her soda. Holding up his glass, he motioned for her to do the same. "To us and the great time we're going to have tonight." They tapped glasses and drank. All the while, her escort stared deeply into her eyes.

I don't even know the man's name . . . and this drink tastes funny.

❄

Running from the train station, Clay flagged a taxi. His next stop? The hotel. After checking in, he dashed to his room, stripped his traveling clothes from his body, and tossed them on the bed. He noticed new clothing hanging neatly in the closet. No time to shower. He was already late.

He grabbed one of the thick wooden hangers from the rod and discovered that it held a suit and a shirt and tie. A tie that was already tied. All he needed to do was slip it over his head and tighten the knot. Looking down to the closet floor, he noticed a pair of dress shoes had been placed directly below the suit. *I remember clothing was mentioned somewhere in the paperwork, but nothing about having my own fashion coordinator.* He wasn't sure he liked that. No, he definitely did not appreciate a stranger choosing the clothing he was to wear.

He dressed quickly and headed for the door, pausing to glance at his reflection in the full-length mirror. His dark hair tapered neatly to his shirt collar, but he kept the hair on top of his head long enough to spike it up with gel or let it fall casually on his forehead when he wished to cover the scar above his right eyebrow. Smiling into the mirror, he admitted he looked darn good. Slapping his cheeks, he said, "It's showtime!"

He was ninety minutes late. Would she still be waiting for him? He had no idea what he'd do if she were gone. Before stepping into the bar, their designated meeting place, he tugged at the tie, took one last look at her photograph and her name, Winn Wahlberg, written on the back, then shoved it deep into his pants' pocket.

He spotted a young woman with long, reddish-blond hair tied back in a tight ponytail and wearing little or no make-up. He thought he recognized her from the photo. But she wasn't alone. Had he made a mistake? Maybe she wasn't the young woman he was here to meet or she became tired of waiting for him and left. He looked around again. No other woman came close to matching her description.

A man, definitely a city guy, was having a drink with her, giving her far too much attention as if she were an exotic specimen. Clay sat at a table that allowed him an inconspicuous view of the young woman and the man at her side. Confused, he watched but saw nothing unusual.

Familiar with pick-up action in a bar—he'd been in plenty of them—what he observed was a guy trying to get lucky with a girl. Clay felt strongly about accomplishing the job he'd been given. Still, he hesitated before interfering. From his vantage point, she seemed to be enjoying herself. He'd watch for a while longer but knew he'd need to crash their party at some point. Nothing would stop him from completing his job successfully.

When she stood, appearing shaky, Clay knew that point had arrived.

"Thanks for the drinks. I'm not feeling well. Will I see you tomorrow?"

The man stood and took her arm. "I'm walking you to your room. I insist."

She pulled away from his grasp, nearly falling. "No. That's not necessary."

Again, he insisted, taking her arm somewhat forcibly, and escorted her to the elevators. Clay stayed close behind, watching the scene unfold in front of him. Something felt wrong. Was this guy a gentleman, or did he have other plans? Time would tell. He watched Winn press the number three button, and the moment the elevator door closed, he bounded up the stairs to the third floor. His gut told him that the young woman he was to escort around Denver for the next five days was in trouble.

He felt a familiar, sudden adrenalin rush as the elevator door opened. Still observing, he saw the couple turn left and walk down the hallway. Shaky, Winn tried a few times before she was able to insert her keycard into the second room from the elevator. The man had one arm around her waist. She looked up at him and clearly said, "Good night." When she said "good night" again, in a much louder, firmer voice, Clay knew she meant it. She'd told the truth about not feeling well. From her tone and unsteadiness, the young woman wanted this guy to leave her alone.

"Hey, what's wrong with you? Can't you see the lady is not interested?" Clay spoke with angry authority as he approached the stranger.

Winn tried to close the door, but the man ignored her discomfort and strong-armed his way into the room.

When Clay heard Winn scream, he picked up speed. In less than a second, he reached the door before it has fully closed and delivered a powerful right hook to the guy's face, knocking him to the floor. Rising slowly to his feet, rubbing his jaw, he said, "Back off, man. I've got work to do here."

Clay wasted no time replying. "I do too, and you're way out of line."

"If you're a cop, arrest this woman. She propositioned me. She's nothing but a cheap, ugly hooker."

That was a lie. This bullying jerk should be arrested for preying on a sweet, unassuming woman. Clay's protective nature turned to rage, letting loose a few more punches before shoving the man out the door. The predator didn't go quietly; he cussed and threatened revenge as he staggered down the hall to the elevators.

Closing the door, Clay locked the deadbolt and turned to see Winn stumble to the bathroom. No doubt about it. She was under the weather. Would she want his help? They were total strangers. He'd give her some space. He turned the TV to a music channel, sat in one of the over-stuffed chairs, and waited. She emerged, wiping her face with a damp washcloth.

"Are you okay? Should I call for a doctor?" he asked, now standing with his hands buried deep in his pockets.

Pale and trembling, she stared at Clay. Dealing with two strange men in one night was justifiably uncomfortable. First, a predator sought her out, then a shining knight without a white horse jumped in to save the day.

"I'm fine. Thank you for your help. You can go now."

"I'm not so sure that's a good idea. You seem kind of shaken."

"Yes, I am. You would be, too, if you'd been set up to be some creepy person's date. Ugh! I should have known better. This whole vacation was too good to be true."

Clay felt blind-sided. His reward had better be worth the complexities facing him. Standing there, unsure of what to say, he hesitated.

Winn slumped down onto the big chair and sighed. "Who are you?"

"I'm Clay Washington, the man assigned to show you around Denver."

Her expression was fraught with skepticism. "Really? I find that difficult to believe. You were supposed to meet me at seven o'clock. How do I know that you are the real guy? The one that The Fantasy Maker chose to teach me about life in the big city?"

He dug out her photo from his pocket. "You look like the woman in the photo I was given. Your name is Winn, right?"

"Most people call me Winn, but my parents call me Winnie. Neither of those is my real name."

"Okay. I was also given an itinerary for the next few days. Proof enough?"

"I suppose so. But you could have found my photo on the Internet. And, if you really are my escort, what's on the itinerary for tonight?"

He took out a sheet of paper from the suit jacket's pocket, unfolded it, and read it to her. "A quick, casual dinner at the Italian restaurant across the street from the hotel, then a movie one block down, followed by some friendly, getting-to-know-each-other conversation at the location of our choice."

"Must we follow the itinerary?" she asked.

Clay didn't know the answer to her question, so he made one up. "No. What do you have in mind?"

"I'm tired and not very hungry. How about a quiet, simple dinner here in my room."

"I can arrange that, but you'll be missing out on your first night in the city."

"That's okay. My city-life fantasy can begin tomorrow."

❄

Winn was unpacking the banged-up, yellow suitcase her mother had loaned her for the trip when she heard a loud pounding on the door. She poked her head from the suite's bedroom and looked toward the door. Instead of opening it, she glanced at Clay. Their eyes locked. Were they thinking the same thing? Winn's heart raced.

Clay must have read her mind or her expression because he said, "That's got to be our dinner. I don't think our bad guy would dare come back." As he stood up and headed for the door, she hoped he was right.

With great relief, Winn watched a smiling woman push in a rolling cart covered with a white tablecloth and a holiday candle. She lifted the protective lids from the entrées allowing the delicious aroma of a steak dinner and a large bowl of chicken noodle soup to escape. Then, she handed Clay the room charge ticket to sign.

"I should sign that. After all, the food came to my room." Winn reached for the ticket, but Clay shook his head, and his mouth formed the word no. She shrugged and sat in the chair he'd pulled out for her.

The woman left, and they ate in silence for a while. Clay devoured his food; Winn slowly sipped her soup.

"Are you feeling any better? Your face has a little more color now."

She felt a jolt zap through her. His comment brought back memories she didn't wish to think about. The sudden look of concern on his face begged for an explanation. *In less than a week, I will never see him again, so what harm could come from confessing a few awkward facts?*

"I don't like to have 'color' on my face. I'm told that I blush often. Sometimes from the heat, sometimes from embarrassment. The reason never mattered, but the people around me, kids and adults alike, took great pleasure in calling me pumpkin face whenever it happened." She looked down at her soup bowl, hoping to avoid any sign of his displeasure or pity.

He reached over the cart and lifted her chin with his fingertips. She could not ignore the kind, thoughtful look in his eyes. The only men that had ever gazed into her eyes were the old and ill patients at the nursing home who needed her help. This was different.

Finally, Clay smiled and broke the silence. "To me, your pretty face is more like," he paused in thought, "the flush of a sunset on snow. Yes. That's how I would describe you."

Speechless and blushing, she took a swallow of water from her glass, buying some time until a response came to mind. "Thank you. That was a nice thing to say."

She wanted to ask if those were his own words or if the company that hired him to be her escort wrote them. She still wondered if he really was the official escort. Wouldn't a hired escort be on time? She had many questions.

Winn pushed her half-empty bowl back; she'd had enough. Clay took her by the hand and led her to a luxurious sofa where they could relax comfortably and continue to get to know each other. She found new energy, her second wind, while Clay's was fading fast.

Her questions poured out. "What do you know about me? Why did you take this job? Is this what you do for a living?"

Clay held up his hand as if to say, STOP! "Whoa, girl. Slow down. I'll try to answer your questions, but I need them to be asked one at a time. How come you're so energetic all of a sudden? It's late for me, and it's been a long day."

"Back at the nursing home, I work the evening shift from three in the afternoon to eleven at night. I'm used to being up and active until midnight. However, mornings are a whole different story."

Clay explained what he could. He'd been told she was from Yuma, Arizona, and had applied for and won a fantasy from The Fantasy Maker organization. He was given a photo so he'd be able to recognize her, and he knew she'd requested a city-life experience.

"Then you are well aware that I did not ask for romance to be part of my fantasy, right?" *Why did I say that?* Quickly, she slid her hands behind her back and crossed her fingers, hoping that small gesture would make her not-quite-truthful comment less egregious.

Clay's eyebrows shot up. "I never really gave that a thought. Now that you mention it, I don't recall seeing *Romance* or *Sex,* not even *Making Out* listed anywhere on the basic itinerary." His serious expression turned into a mischievous grin. "But would that be listed?"

Feeling the color rising on her face again, she said, "Let's move on. So, you're a Denver escort? Is that what you do for a living?"

"That's what I'm doing this week."

His answer was far too flimsy. What was he hiding? He was not only gloriously handsome, but he'd saved her from a man with bad intentions. Still, something didn't feel right. *What have I gotten myself into?* She thought for the second time tonight.

Then it came to her. She gasped and blurted out, "You! You're The Fantasy Maker."

He stood up and briskly walked across the room, catching his foot on the leg of a chair. Regaining his balance, he turned and replied, "Maybe, maybe not. What I can tell you is this: I am here to assist you with your city-life experience and make sure you enjoy your fantasy vacation."

Winn watched him walk toward the door that led to the hallway.

"So, what's the plan?" she asked.

He leaned his back against the door. "Come a little closer, and I'll tell you."

Without any hesitation, she stepped closer and stood a mere twelve inches from his lean body. He took her hands in his and whispered, "Tomorrow will be a long and busy day. Lock your door, set the deadbolt, and get some sleep." He kissed the back of each hand, tapped the end of her nose lightly with his finger, and left.

Winn followed his instructions, but she could not sleep.

Chapter Two

December 14

Clay, a morning person, looked up from the cart containing their breakfast to see a startled but sleepy-eyed version of Winn wearing a flannel nightgown. "You're in my room," she said.

"Good observation. Look! I've brought breakfast."

"Back up just a second. You have a key to my room?"

"Of course not. But, by some coincidence, we have adjoining rooms. See?" He pointed to the door that connected them.

"You're already dressed. You sure take good care of your clothes. Did you iron that crease in those slacks?"

He changed the subject. "Let's eat. After some food and a lot of coffee, we'll talk about clothes."

Winn must have been famished because she ate

everything on her plate, the scrambled eggs, the potatoes O'Brien, the toast, the bacon, and the fruit.

"What's on today's itinerary?"

"Shopping." He'd be glad when this day was over. He'd never shopped with a woman for clothing before. Never! He felt awkward even before their excursion began.

"What are you shopping for?" she asked, with a confused look on her face.

"It seems someone has already shopped for me." He caught himself before elaborating on his clothing situation. "This is your day to shop for a complete uptown wardrobe."

"I wouldn't know where to start, where to go, what to get—"

"No problem. I know exactly where to start. Go throw some clothes on. Anything will do. You won't be wearing your Yuma clothing after our first stop. You're a city girl this week, remember?"

They'd visited one boutique shop and one high-end department store by lunchtime. Winn left the first shop wearing tan designer wool slacks and a luscious rust-colored sweater that brought out the green in her eyes. Deciding between two silk blouses that looked the same to Clay, she chose the cream-colored one. Their next stop was Nordstrom.

The Christmas windows at Nordstrom were beyond belief even for Clay. Winn seemed mesmerized by the elaborate decorations and stared at them until Clay nudged her toward the door. Inside, a trio of strolling musicians played Christmas music, and a giant Christmas tree mounted on a turning floor spun slowly. Winn craned her neck to see the top of the tree that held the most beautiful gold star with twinkling white lights on each point. She clapped her hands in delight, causing Clay to laugh out loud at her excitement.

Clay paced within close proximity to the dressing room. Each time Winn tried on something, she'd come out, do a pirouette and ask whether he approved. By the time they left the casual wear department, they were carrying huge bags of clothing plus a few outfits on hangers.

Choosing shoes was next on the agenda. They purchased one pair of flat shoes for walking, a pair of low-heeled boots to look stylish, plus one pair of black leather high-heeled shoes for dressing up.

Clay didn't know if he'd make it through the day and was relieved when Winn mentioned she had far more clothing than she needed for her week in the city. He wished it were that simple.

"Are we done yet?" Winn asked with weariness in her voice.

They'd purchased more than they could carry. Before answering her, Clay took out his cell phone. He'd been given a phone number to call anytime they needed transportation above and beyond the travel mentioned in their itinerary. They didn't need a ride, but their packages did. Five minutes later, they waved goodbye to the limo driver transporting Winn's new wardrobe to the hotel.

"To answer your question, we're not done. We've only just begun. Now that your bags are on their way to the hotel, we'll grab some lunch and continue shopping." He laughed when he saw her eyes widen with amazement. But he had a job to do, and he needed to do it well.

They had a quick meal at a small restaurant. After lunch, they purchased cold-weather gear and dressy attire for the gala evening events on their schedule. A few more pairs of high-fashion shoes were added to Winn's wardrobe.

"This is too much. I don't need even half the things we purchased today."

"I do understand, but this is your fantasy vacation, so you might as well enjoy everything it has to offer."

"I suppose you're right; it just seems extreme."

The sun dipped below the tops of the skyscrapers surrounding them, causing the temperature to drop rapidly. Arm in arm, they picked up their pace and headed to the hotel. One more city block and they could relax for a while. A short while. They were expected at The Neon Disco at nine that evening. They needed to shower, change into the proper attire, and eat dinner before hailing a cab to their evening destination.

Clay stopped and turned around. "Did you see that guy?"

"Which guy? There are dozens of men on this sidewalk."

"That rhinestone cowboy. A totally fake country boy. Oh, sure. His Tony Lama boots are worthy, but the rest? Just a costume."

"And how do you, Mr. City Guy, know all that?"

Flustered by his mistake, he searched for the right words to say. He'd already said too much. During her fantasy week, he was to play the part of an authentic, sophisticated city dweller, not a Kansas farm boy. This job, the charade, was more challenging than he expected. Winn was a sweet young woman, and lying to her didn't sit well with his principles.

"Just a guess, really. He was way too clean. Everything looked new. And I saw those boots in a magazine on my way to Denver."

"I thought you lived here. You're not making sense this afternoon, Clay."

A police SUV and a fire truck, followed by an ambulance, zoomed by with lights flashing and sirens blasting, making a response impossible. *Ah. Saved by someone else's misfortune.*

Riding up in the elevator, Clay glanced at the remaining items on today's itinerary. He had mixed feelings about the details it provided. He never would've thought of doing the tasks listed. In fact, he'd rather not perform some of them at all.

His duties, at the moment, consisted of helping Winn unpack and organize all of today's purchases.

Really? Then, after showing her what he'd be wearing to the disco, choose the outfit she'd wear tonight. *Good grief!* This job was getting too weird, bordering on bizarre. He wished he'd seen these daily itineraries before accepting the deal that would eventually lead to his own fantasy. Still, he would have taken the job, but at least he'd have been mentally prepared for what was to come. Shopping consultant and wardrobe coordinator was never mentioned.

With her new outfits hung neatly in the closet and the shoes lined up on the closet floor, Winn fell back on the queen-size bed and laughed until her sides ached. Her fantasy felt more like a modern fairy tale. Though undeniably handsome and extremely well-dressed, her prince charming baffled her with his awkwardness. She asked herself, what was wrong with this picture, and was determined to find out. In the meantime, she'd enjoy her time in the city with her personal tour guide.

She heard the anticipated knock on the door between their suites. Clay used that door exclusively but had agreed to honor her request to knock before entering. In retrospect, she should have made sure he understood that he needed to wait until she invited him in. Live and learn. And, when it came to men, she had much to learn.

He hovered at the bedroom door with a clothes-filled hanger in his hand before she'd managed to rise up from her daydreaming position on the bed. "These are my clothes for tonight."

Why was he so concerned about their clothing? Maybe he worked for a designer. Puzzled, she walked over to him, saying, "Looks good. Whatever you want to wear is fine with me." Did he need her approval? That didn't make sense for a sophisticated man about town.

Instead of leaving to get dressed, he told her, "I think that short black dress would be a good choice for you to wear tonight. What do you think?"

"You're placing far too much importance on clothing. That's what I think."

"You're right. Can you be dressed and ready to go out in about forty-five minutes?"

"I can be ready in ten. See you then." He looked shocked as she gently pushed him through the door and back into his own suite.

Precisely as she'd told him, she was ready in ten minutes. All she had to do was pull the silky, stretchy, little black dress over her head, tug it down—it was shorter than any dress she'd ever worn—then step into the black heels. As far as she was concerned, she was good to go after a few practice steps in the unfamiliar footwear. Feeling energized, she chuckled at the naughty thought that came to mind. Two could play the knock-and-enter game.

She knocked and entered. Shocked to see Clay undressed, she averted her eyes. "Oh, sorry. I thought you'd at least have your pants on by now." She turned away from the gorgeous, muscular man with an incredible tan, wearing only his boxer shorts. Exercising could explain the muscles, but the tan? How did he spend his time when he wasn't escorting women around Denver? She'd find out before the night was over.

"You weren't joking when you said you'd be ready in ten minutes. I was looking to see if I had another pair of black pants. The ones I was going to wear were too skinny and tight."

"Didn't you try them on before you bought them?"

"Uh, I must have forgotten to do that. I'll figure something out. Don't worry. If you would, please go back to your suite. I'll be ready in five minutes."

She shrugged and stole one more curious look at him. "All right."

Five minutes wasn't enough time to begin one of the new audiobooks she'd brought along, so she picked up the only paperback book she had with her and opened it up to where she'd left a yellow highlighter clipped to a page. Though the book appeared tattered and dog-eared, it was still her favorite. Winn located and finished highlighting the word *rhinestone* when Clay walked through the adjoining door without knocking.

"I'm ready," he said. "What? Why are you looking at me that way?"

"Didn't we agree to knock"?

"But you were expecting me." He smiled, his perfect

white teeth sparkling. "Are you ready for your first night on the town?"

Nodding, she grabbed her new sequin, cross-body bag, and the soft wool coat, which Clay took from her hands and proceeded to help her slip into. "I can do that myself, you know," she protested.

"Yes, I know," he whispered into her ear. "But tonight and for the next five days, you will be treated like a lady. Fantasy or no fantasy, you deserve it." His hands lingered on her shoulders.

She enjoyed the musky scent of his cologne and the warmth of his breath tickling her neck. Had the city-life aspect of her fantasy taken a backseat to romance? Would he even consider a little flirtation with her? She wished she'd included that as part of her requested fantasy. Most likely, it was not in his job description. He had been hired to show her around Denver. She was nothing more than an assignment to him, a temporary job.

"Let's go," he said, his voice filled with joy, his face all smiles as if he were thrilled to be taking Winn to dinner, then dancing at a disco. *Maybe he loves to dance.*

They began the short walk to the elevator. Winn looked over her shoulder, sensing something, hearing something, but didn't know what. She shrugged it off and convinced herself that huge hotel buildings probably creaked and groaned now and then.

Clay must have noticed her movements or expression because he asked, "Did you leave something back in your room?"

"No," she said, reaching out to press the down arrow rather than offer an explanation.

He beat her to the button and pressed the up arrow, stating that their dinner reservation was at the restaurant on the eighteenth floor. Smiling dreamily down at her, he said, "There was a hand-written note on today's list of activities, and it mentioned that this is THE best restaurant in town."

As they stepped from the elevator, a man dressed in a tuxedo greeted them. "Ms. Wahlberg, Mr. Washington. Our best and most requested table has been reserved for you. Follow me, please."

Winn felt a slight movement under her feet. Looking straight ahead, she saw floor-to-ceiling windows. Excited, she realized she was standing in a rotating restaurant, something she'd heard of but couldn't imagine! During dinner, she would see a magnificent 360-degree view of the city's lights. Thrilled, it took all of her composure to keep from jumping for joy like a game show winner. When they were seated at their table, which was a mere inch from the floor to ceiling window, she looked into Clay's eyes, and her words spilled out. "This is the best night of my life! The most . . . Clay? Clay! What's the matter?"

Under the faint, twinkling white lights on the ceiling of the dining room, Clay looked unusually pale with a greenish pallor. His eyes were focused on the empty plate in front of him, and his flashy, warm smile was nowhere to be seen.

"Are you all right?"

"I'll be fine," he mumbled, still staring at his plate.

Winn's attention turned back to gazing down at the city. "Can you believe this view? Look how small everything is. Buildings look like tiny houses, and the cars look like toys. I'm not sure I can see people unless that's what the tiny dots are."

She begged Clay to look at the view. Why wouldn't he look? A server came by with a bottle of wine. Her concerns for Clay were temporarily interrupted as she watched the man fill their glasses. When he left, she leaned forward and whispered to Clay, "I'm not twenty-one. What if he asks for my ID?"

"He won't."

Clay remained on edge throughout dinner, refusing to enjoy the view of the night sky and the city below. His behavior was baffling. Winn patted his hand, attempted to engage him in conversation, and offered tastes of her entrée, but all efforts to comfort him failed. He barely touched his food. When the dessert menu was given to them, he said, "No thanks, the check, please." He signed the bill to his room and said, "Let's go."

Once in the elevator, his color improved. By the time they were at street level, he'd returned to his wonderful self.

"Next stop, The Neon Disco, the hottest spot in Denver. We'll need to take a taxi."

In fifteen minutes, they were inside the disco, surrounded by multicolor flashing lights and loud, thumping music. The gorgeous, well-dressed people looked more like movie stars than Denver locals. Winn felt twinges of intimidation and was certain she was the one with a greenish-looking face now.

They found a high-top table for two. Clay ordered a Coors for himself and a Coke for Winn. "Do you feel like dancing?" he asked.

She shook her head. "Maybe later," she lied. "I'm fascinated watching everyone." The school dances back in Yuma were nothing like this. She'd look like a fool trying to emulate these sophisticated partiers with their slick, high-energy dance steps. Sitting on the barstool was more her speed.

After an hour of people watching, she was ready to leave. Clay was too. But then the DJ played a slow song, and suddenly she was in Clay's arms swaying to the music. No fancy steps required. None performed. *I may be a plain, small-town girl, but right now, I'd lay odds that I am happier than any other woman on the dance floor.*

Chapter Three

December 15

Clay tossed and turned, unable to sleep. He kept thinking of his embarrassment when he'd been caught off guard, betrayed by his own body. His fear of heights messed with his mind and ego, producing an uncomfortable feeling of anxiety. Had Winn figured out his problem? He wasn't sure. She'd been noticeably attentive, but that made the charade, the pretending to be someone other than himself, more troubling.

Lying did not sit well with him. In the past, he'd done things he wasn't proud of, such as leading women on, heading off to college instead of helping out at the family farm, and, of course, fighting, but he wasn't a liar. It never occurred to him that the woman he'd escort around town would be so adorable or her naivety and sweetness would be the fly in the ointment. He flipped his pillow to the cool side and begged for sleep to come.

Relaxing in the luxurious bed, Winn pressed the STOP button on her compact CD player. She'd already listened to thirty minutes of her audiobook, *The Brothers Karamazov* by Dostoyevsky, to help pass the time. Where was Clay? He was the morning person, not her, and he was the man with the plan.

She took a shower, which included washing her hair and scrubbing her face. Wide awake, she dried off with the most oversized towel she'd ever laid eyes on. She pulled her hair into its usual, tight ponytail and dressed in a pair of gray slacks, the boots with two-inch heels, a pink silk blouse, and the lavender cardigan sweater. *Ready or not, here I come.*

She knocked on the door and waited for Clay's invitation to enter. She knocked again.

"Clay?" No response. Curious and worried, she went in. The door to his bedroom was closed, his clothing from the previous night scattered on the sofa. A sheet of paper on the coffee table caught her attention. She was not a snooper and wouldn't touch it, but her curiosity caused her to glance toward it.

From where she stood, she could tell it was a list typed on letterhead. Across the top of the paper were four words. She needed to get closer to decipher those words. Reading 'the' was easy; the other words presented a challenge. Against her better judgment, she picked up the sheet of paper and held it in front of her face.

Seconds later, Clay emerged from his bedroom, sleep still in his eyes. A sudden alertness came over him when he saw what she was holding. Strange. He looked worried and upset. Why would he be worried? Angry, sure, but worried, no way. After all, she was the one who had stepped over the line and invaded his privacy.

"Winn, I'm sorry I overslept. You shouldn't have seen today's updated information. I had strict instructions to keep all communication from The Friendly Escort Service from you. Your days here in Denver with me should feel natural and spontaneous, rather than meticulously planned."

Clay had no way of knowing she hadn't read the entire itinerary. She hadn't gotten beyond the first word, but several questions came to mind now.

"You were hired by a company called The Friendly Escort Service? I thought The Fantasy Maker arranged everything for me."

Clay took possession of the problematic paper she still held in her hands. Silent, appearing to be thinking, he finally said, "Let me get dressed. We'll forgo the first two activities on the list. That will give us a chance to talk. Okay with you?"

"Sure." And though she had no idea what activities she just gave up, talking was a good idea. Knowing more about this fantasy situation she'd gotten herself into would be helpful. And she was anxious to learn a lot more about Clay. A knock at the door followed by "Room Service!" put an end to her thoughts. Clay was in the bedroom, so she opened the door and signed her name to the check. At least breakfast wasn't one of the activities deleted from the list.

"That smells good," Clay said a few minutes later when he walked into the sitting room dressed smartly for the day. They devoured the meal in awkward silence. Was each one waiting for the other to speak? No words came, but Clay stood up and went into Winn's suite. He returned, carrying her warm coat, gloves, and the cute hat she'd selected at Nordstrom. "Let's walk and talk. Though the sky is blue, the temp is below freezing. You'll need these."

He, too, dressed warmly. Once down the elevator and out the hotel's front door, Clay took her hand. They'd walked about four blocks when they came to a street vendor selling coffee and hot chocolate. Clay purchased one of each. At first, the drinks were too hot, but they were just right by the time they sat on a bench in City Park.

"Tell me the story of Winn. I want to know all about you and how you ended up in a fantasy not far from the Rocky Mountains."

She'd hoped he'd be the one to tell all first, but that was not going to happen. So, with one hand twisting the end of her long ponytail that was sticking out of the woolen hat and the other holding the warm cup of hot chocolate, she began.

"I'm a caregiver at the Sunnydale Nursing Home in Yuma. Marie, one of the patients, showed me an advertisement in a caregivers' magazine for a free vacation. She's too weak to walk and spends most of the daytime hours in a wheelchair, but her mind is still brilliant. She read all of the information to me, which gave her something to do and made her happy, so I let her help me apply."

Clay frowned. "You applied to win a free vacation? Not a fantasy?"

"That's right. The ad said, 'Are you a hardworking caregiver? A well-deserved, all- expense-paid vacation is waiting for you.' All we had to do was send in my name, date of birth, and place of employment." The following day, with help from Marie and the use of the facility's computer, Winn applied. She remembered laughing at the thought of a vacation. What would she do with time away from work or away from home?

Sighing, Winn continued. "I hadn't heard of The Fantasy Maker until the day I received the notification stating I was a finalist. I'd never been so excited in my life. When I saw all the paperwork this Fantasy Maker person required regarding my fantasy, I became skeptical. I came very close to throwing it all in the trash. But I didn't, I was chosen, and here I am."

"That's quite a story, Miss Winn. It took courage to agree to such an adventure."

"I suppose so. I'm curious about how you were selected to be my escort. Is The Friendly Escort Service based here in Denver?"

Clay hesitated, and his foot tapped rapidly on the sidewalk. "I think that is a nationwide company, and The Fantasy Maker is just one of their accounts. I'm not privy to all the details, but I'm very happy to be your escort."

Winn was slow at reading words, but she was fast when it came to reading people. She felt certain that, deep down, Clay was a wonderful man, but she was just as certain he was not telling her the truth.

According to the details left that morning, tonight was dress-up night. Clay would wear a tuxedo, and Winn would be decked out in a long, black silky dress. That much he already knew. He'd been given the basic itinerary before arriving in Denver, but it lacked the specifics of each day. Someone always managed to slip the current day's details under the door while he slept. As an early riser, he'd study these notes before each day with Winn began, except today.

A limo was scheduled to pick them up at 7:15 p.m. Clay looked at his watch. It was five minutes past five. He started getting ready early, not knowing how long it would take him to put on his dressy duds. Without knocking, he opened the adjoining door. "Hey, Winn?

We need to be downstairs, dressed in our finest. A limo will pick us up in a couple of hours."

"Where will this limo take us?" She smiled and seemed more comfortable with the idea of fancy clothes and a limo ride than he was.

"First to a restaurant, then to the theater. Apparently, there's a special performance of a highly rated musical not available to the general public until next week." His comments were based on what he remembered from his *detailed* itinerary. Still, he had no idea what he was talking about. The evening's events would be a surprise for both of them.

Winn was excited about seeing what might be a preview of a Broadway production. "I'm going to soak in the tub for a while. Come back as soon as you're dressed. Can I assume this is the night I wear the long black dress and the short faux fur jacket?"

He nodded and returned to his suite. Once in his bedroom, he hit the power button on the TV's remote and found a sports channel. Football. A good distraction from anticipating the formal evening that lay ahead of him. Would Winn be able to adapt to such an evening? She was far less worldly than he was. At least he'd graduated from college, had visited several states, and had worked a variety of jobs. She'd never left Yuma.

Dressed in his tux with its accessories and shiny black shoes, he threw his topcoat over his arm and entered Winn's suite. Not seeing her in the sitting area, he called out loudly, "It's me. I'm back."

She came out of the bedroom in the plush bathrobe provided by the hotel, her hair tied back as tightly as ever. Obviously, not ready to go. That was okay. They had half an hour before the limo would arrive. "I just need to slip into the dress. I'll be back in a flash."

Clay shook his head. He'd known when he first laid eyes on her that she was a pleasant-looking female. And after he got to know her better, he had a hunch there was a beautiful woman behind the totally unadorned face, and tight, flat hair pulled back in a ponytail. Even a gorgeous woman would be challenged to look terrific under those circumstances. Someday he'd ask her why she always wore her hair like that.

"Clay," she called loudly. "My hair tie broke. Can you bring my purse in here? That's where I keep extra ties."

"Sure thing." He found her bag without any trouble and headed first into her bedroom, then into the bathroom-dressing area. "Here you—oh, sorry. I thought you'd be in that black dress by now." He couldn't stop staring. There she stood, wearing only her baby-blue panties and matching bra. Her long red hair tumbled down over her shoulders in loose waves. What he'd imagined about her appearance had suddenly come true right before his eyes. All it took was a broken hair tie. Amazing! She was beautiful, and he told her so.

He should have let it go at that, but he didn't. "Why do you wear your hair tied back so tightly? Doesn't that give you a headache?"

"I never think about my hairstyle. I need it out of the way, especially at work." Tears came to her eyes. "Then there's my mother. She'd squash any form of vanity or primping. It wasn't allowed. I couldn't even use a tinted Chapstick without feeling guilty."

That explained a lot. Clay couldn't believe any parent would be so strict. "You're not at home now. There is no one here to place any restrictions on you. So, you can let your hair down." He wanted to say more, but a knock on the door of her suite interrupted his words.

"Can you get that, Clay?"

A beautiful woman wearing a white smock stood at the door. She carried a case resembling a toolbox. "I'm here to help Winn prepare for tonight's gala event. Compliments of The Fantasy Maker."

"Uh, sure. Come on in. I'll let her know you're here." He hurried back to the dressing area. "It seems your Fantasy Maker has sent someone, a woman, to help you get ready. Are you okay with that? I'm pretty sure it will involve primping."

Winn's eyebrows shot up. "Well, that's unexpected, but I suppose most fantasies contain unexpected things. Send her in. But stay close by in case I need you."

He sat in the sitting area, turned her TV on, and waited. Fifteen minutes later, the woman came out smiling. "She's all yours and ready to go. Have fun!" She waved and left.

Winn walked into the room. It took a moment for Clay to catch his breath, but then he said, "Wow! First, you were the nicest person I'd ever met, and now you are also the most beautiful woman I have ever seen in my entire life. Did you look at yourself? You're to-die-for gorgeous."

Tears welled up in her eyes. Clay produced a linen handkerchief and dabbed carefully at the dampness. "Please tell me those are tears of joy."

She nodded. "They are. All my life, people told me I was plain and unattractive. That woman showed me a few simple tricks with mascara, liner, powder, and lip color. That's all it took."

"I'm not surprised. I never thought you were plain or unattractive. Not only are you beautiful on the outside, but you're beautiful on the inside." Clay couldn't take his eyes off this beautiful woman who stood before him. Taking her arm, he said, "Let's go catch our limo and see what else this night brings."

"Where are we going first? Do you know the name of the restaurant?" Winn tended to ask multiple questions all at once. It was becoming her trademark.

"It's called The Wharf. I've never been there, but it got great reviews, and it's close to the theater."

"That is an odd name for a land-locked restaurant," Winn said, looking perplexed and confident at the same time.

"Really? Why do you say that?"

She had an immediate answer. "When I imagine a wharf, it is on the coast where boats, even ships, load and unload their passengers or cargo."

"You're sounding like a dictionary."

"Well, that is my favorite book," Winn said, looking directly into his eyes.

"Huh. Maybe the restaurant's décor has an ocean theme and serves fish. We will soon find out. Let's go. I'm starving."

"Me too."

The limo driver parked close to the front entrance, got out, and opened the door for Winn. Clay let himself out and was at Winn's side in no time.

In a way, they were both correct. The interior resembled the inside of a old wooden pirate ship. And through the fake windows, painted on the walls, diners could see lots of ocean on one side of the restaurant and part of a wharf on the other.

"Follow me, please," said a nautically costumed host. He led them to a long table at the front of the large, ship-shaped room. "You'll be dining at the captain's table tonight, mates. Enjoy your dinner."

As they were seated, Winn giggled. "Do you think Captain Hook will be joining us?"

Before Clay came up with a reply, a man and woman reached across the narrow table, presumably to shake hands.

"Captain Bligh, here. Welcome to my ship."

Looking at each other, speechless for a moment, all Winn and Clay could say was, "Thank you."

The woman with Captain Bligh added, "Your server will be with you momentarily. How about starting with two mugs of rum?"

"Bring 'em on," Clay said.

The captain and his lady left, and Winn felt free to react to their unusual dining situation. "Are we really going to drink two mugs of rum? You know I'm not twenty-one yet?"

"No one here is going to care about that minor detail. And, we don't need to drink any of it. I do think we should at least pretend to. You know, get in the mood, give it a go since we're dining on a pirate ship."

"I like your idea."

The mugs of rum arrived quickly. When that wench-looking server turned to hurry away, Winn asked to see a menu.

"Oh, the captain has chosen your dinners for this evening, but it's okay if you'd rather order from a menu yourself."

Both Clay and Winn shrugged. "We'll take what your captain has chosen for us." Clay said.

"In that case, I have only one question for you," the server said. "Would you like your main entre with or without its head?"

"I'll take the whole darn thing." Clay's reply shocked Winn.

"Headless, please," Winn said, wishing now she'd asked for a menu.

The captain stood in the center of his ship, and his lady tapped on a bell capturing everyone's attention. "Cheers to all of you, the best darn crew I've ever had. Raise your mugs to the sky and repeat after me. No land in sight . . . no land in sight. No mutiny tonight . . . no mutiny tonight. Down the hatch . . . Down the hatch. Or you'll walk the plank," the captain snarled.

"That was fun, different, and exhausting," Winn said once they were back in the comfort and quiet of the limo. "The food was excellent, and I was pleasantly surprised that our main course consisted of rainbow trout. I half expected some sort of sea creature."

Clay agreed with her comments and added, "But we were definitely overdressed for that event. Now, I wonder if our theater experience will be unusual too."

"I'm excited to see a live theatrical performance. I know I will love it no matter how unusual it may be."

The marquee came into view. "Look at that, Winn," Clay pointed at the marquee, which displayed the play's title. Up in lights were the words: LITTLE RED: a musical. "I guess there will be some singing."

"Oh, my gosh. Look at the long line, Clay. We do have tickets for this event, right?"

"I don't personally have the tickets with me. Just the itinerary."

"With this crowd, I'd feel a whole lot better if our tickets were in your pocket or wallet," Winn sighed and hoped everything would work out.

The limo driver pulled up and stopped right in front of the theater's main entrance. He opened the door for Clay while another tuxedoed man opened Winn's door for her. That man escorted them through the entrance and the lobby and down the aisle to their center stage, front row seats. Not once were they asked for their tickets.

Hearing the commotion of the theater patrons hurrying to their seats, Winn turned to take a look. "Clay, are we over-dressed for this event too?"

"No, I'm sure we're dressed appropriately. Why do you ask?"

"It feels like everyone is looking at us."

"In a way, that makes sense. After all, we arrived in a limo and were ushered in ahead of most of the others waiting in line. And, we look fantastic!"

The house lights dimmed, and music began to play. Clay held Winn's hand and whispered, "It's showtime. Here we go."

They had a blast watching this incredibly creative version of Little Red Ridinghood. Clay was correct. There was a lot of singing and occasional audience participation when specific sound effects were asked for. A gardening grandma, a forest in danger, and a whole bunch of new characters were part of this performance. The cast received a standing ovation at the end.

After the cast left the stage and patrons headed toward the exits, Little Red came skipping back out. "I almost forgot. Winn and Clay," she projected, "the Wolf and I would like the pleasure of your company back-stage." She pointed to a staircase and waved them over.

Everyone, still in costume, greeted them as if they were celebrities. Champagne flowed, and they all ate some of the Opening Night luscious cake.

Exhausted from their busy day, Clay and Winn were ready to return to their hotel. They thanked the cast, said goodbye, and wished them good luck on future performances.

Back in the limo, Clay said quietly, "The Fantasy Maker went all out on tonight's events. I wonder how much our backstage visit added to the total."

"This was an amazing evening. One I will never forget, and I'm so happy we had these experiences together."

"Which did you enjoy more? Captain Bligh or Little Red?" Clay asked.

"I cannot answer your question. The two events are incomparable."

They dozed off with their heads together during the ride back to the hotel.

Chapter Four

December 16

The morning light shone brightly through the sheer curtains in Winn's bedroom. She must have slept in. Where was Clay? Mr. Early Riser should have been up by now, demanding she eat a good breakfast and informing her of their plans for the day. Wrapped in the plush robe, she grabbed a bottle of orange juice from the mini-bar. Moving to the sofa, she enjoyed the view of the clear blue sky and the wide-open spaces visible in the distance. Not a cloud in sight. No snow in the forecast, just freezing cold temperatures.

Her thoughts shifted from the weather to last night with Clay. She couldn't have felt more like Cinderella if she'd been wearing glass slippers. The evening was wonderful, magical—too good to be true. Perhaps that was the definition of a fantasy.

Falling for her escort was not in the plan, but that's what was happening. She sighed deeply, accepting there was no way he'd fall for her. Not a handsome city guy who could have any woman he chose. The fun they were having was a job for him, something he did too well.

If she didn't calm down, take a step back, and get real, there'd be no smile on her face when she boarded the homebound plane. She'd hate sitting on the plane with tears rolling down her cheeks. What could be more embarrassing? Somewhere she'd heard, 'To worry about what you don't have is to waste what you do have.' Instead of feeling sad about leaving Clay in a few days, she would focus on enjoying the city and be thankful she had a wonderful escort to show her around. That was that.

"A penny for your thoughts."

Startled from her reverie, Winn looked up. "Hi. I didn't hear you come in."

"I can tell. You were thinking deeply about something probably worth way more than a penny."

His smile was infectious, even though every inch of him screamed out: I'm a slick, well-dressed city boy just doing his job.

"What are we doing today?"

"We are touring the city, mostly on foot. So we need to dress warmly. Fortunately, the weather forecast calls for unseasonably warm temperatures and lots of sun."

"Then why are we dressing warmly?"

Clay laughed out loud. "Because 'unseasonably warm' this time of year at this altitude means part of the day will be above freezing instead of below freezing. Temperatures rise when the sun is high enough in the sky so the tall buildings no longer block its warming light."

"I get it. That's still pretty cold."

Clay nodded. "Are you hungry?"

"Starving!"

"Our first stop will be at one of the semi-famous street vendors. That's where we'll get a bite of breakfast. Hope you don't mind eating while standing."

She laughed. "What could be more fun than standing on a street corner, almost freezing, and eating something we will call *breakfast*? I hope it's more than a bite. After the fun we had last night, I'm so hungry I think I could eat a grand slam breakfast from Denny's all by myself."

Winn dressed in a hurry. When she walked out of the bedroom, Clay laughed. "You look like you're going to Alaska."

"To me, coming from Yuma, this is Alaska."

"C'mon, Miss Alaska. Let's go."

They stopped at an outdoor stand where they each chose a jumbo, hot and salty pretzel and a cup of steaming coffee. The fast, convenient food allowed Clay and Winn to walk and eat at the same time. It was still too chilly to sit or stand still. They'd find something more substantial to eat later in the day.

They had an hour before the Denver Art Museum, their first official destination, would open its doors. Walking up and down busy streets taking in the sounds of traffic and the smells coming from Rosenberg's Bagels was a wonderful experience for Winn. That one hour flew by.

At the museum, they lost track of time while moving from gallery to gallery studying the paintings. Clay told her they were overdue for their lunch reservation, so they picked up brown bag lunches from a street vendor and ate them sitting in the sun on a park bench.

"We have outdoor vendors in Yuma too. They're not just a city thing, you know."

"We'll eat a real city meal tonight. For now, eat your hot dog." He tried, unsuccessfully, to stifle his laughter.

While eating, Winn noticed Clay had an extraordinary talent. He could engage in conversation with squirrels and birds. *I'd love to have a video of this.* The animals tilted their heads as if listening to his words and then replied with chirps and chatters.

Continuing their self-guided tour of Denver, they saw a multi-breed dog rescue group set up at the far end of City Park. Without speaking a word, they veered from the sidewalk toward the dogs. Some dogs slept, others yapped. A few were high-spirited, while others looked forlorn. Clay looked at the dogs longingly. He spoke to each one, telling Winn he'd never had a dog but always wanted one. Anytime the subject came up, his father was adamant that wasn't going to happen. Winn's family fed the feral cats that hung around their home. That seemed to satisfy her family's slender need for an animal.

They petted several dogs and held a few fluffy puppies. Who could resist a puppy? Lala, a woman from the group, did her best to convince them to adopt one of the dogs. "A nice couple like you would be perfect parents for one of our dogs. Today, the fees have been lowered so much that these dogs are practically free." Her green eyes sparkled, her shiny red lips smiled, and her whole face glowed.

Winn's nurturing side wanted to help a dog, but her practical side won out. "I'm from out of state and will fly home in a couple of days. Sorry. There is no way I can take any of these dogs." Then she looked at Clay. "But this guy can. He lives in the Denver area." The panicked look on his face put a smile on hers. Hadn't he just said that he'd always wanted a dog?

Clay struggled with his answer. "Uh, my high-rise apartment is small, and I'm never home. It wouldn't work." He looked at Winn, then at Lala, as if wanting their approval.

Lala said, "I understand. Just know we're here often should your situation change."

Reaching into her bag, Winn removed a fifty-dollar bill from her wallet. She hadn't yet spent any of the cash provided by The Fantasy Maker. A donation to the dog rescue lightened her mood. She always felt good when doing something to help others. Clay matched her donation.

Satisfied by their actions, they agreed it was time to head back to the hotel. They said their goodbyes to the dog rescue staff, who thanked them again for their generosity. Approaching the outer edge of the display of homeless animals, they noticed a cage housing one sad-looking black dog with floppy ears. Attached to that cage was a hand-written sign with the words, LAST CHANCE. They were drawn to this lonely creature immediately. Clay and Winn felt a connection to the dog and agreed there was something special about it.

Winn waved and called out, "Lala, what does Last Chance mean?"

The woman hurried over and explained the dog had issues and didn't get along with anyone. No one wanted him, and his time with the rescue had run out. "If no one takes him today, I'm afraid his life is over." She shook her head, and the glow disappeared from her face.

Clay and Winn looked at each other with horror in their eyes. Winn knelt down next to the cage. The dog cautiously sniffed her. There was movement in its tail, slow at first, but soon that tail wagged vigorously, making circles in the air. Clay took his glove off and bent down to let the dog sniff his hand and was surprised when he received an enthusiastic lick.

Clay asked, "Can you let him out of the cage?"

"I wouldn't advise it. Like I said, he's got issues, especially with men."

Winn knelt beside Clay, who began talking to this poor dog caged up on doggie death row. Looking toward Lala, he asked, "What's his name?"

"He didn't come with a name, so he was assigned a number. He's number 27."

"Let him out of the damn cage. If he doesn't bite me, we're taking him." He looked at Winn. "If that's okay with you."

Though shocked by his angry tone, she nodded her approval. "Let's see what happens."

Lala tenuously opened the cage, apprehension written on her face. Number 27 leaped at Clay with such force, the dog nearly knocked him over. That leap might look like an attack from a distance, but up close, it was pure enthusiasm.

After licking Clay's face, the dog jumped over to Winn and put his paw on her thigh, asking her to pet him. It was love at first sight. Fate at work. After several minutes of watching this dog-that-liked-no-one jump from Clay to Winn, tears spilled from Lala's eyes. "It's a miracle. I knew you two were the perfect couple to give a dog a home. I just didn't think it would be this one."

Looking into each other's eyes, Winn spoke first. "We can't let him die."

"No, we can't. Somehow, we'll give Number 27 a new life and a new name."

The two well-dressed humans and the rambunctious dog with a ragged rope for a leash received many odd looks as they walked around the city searching for a pet store. Eventually, they found one, not a big box store but a boutique.

Clay carried the bag containing gourmet, grain-free dog food, as well as food and water dishes. Winn's bag held dog shampoo, a brush, and some treats. Number 27 proudly wore a new collar connected to a fine leather leash. Fairly soon, the odd looks at the threesome lessened.

Nearing the hotel, the reality of their decision began to sink in. No pets except service dogs were allowed, and Winn would be back home in Yuma, Arizona, in less than two days. Taking the dog was not wise, but they had agreed it was the only choice. Neither was willing to let this dog be put down. Sneaking the dog up to their suites was their first challenge. Tonight, they'd have a serious and strategic conversation.

A few seconds later, Clay announced, "I've got a plan."

They circled the hotel hoping to find an alternate, seldom-used entrance with a staircase inside. Once they found such a door, Clay and the dog would enter, dash up the stairs, and, hopefully, not be seen by hotel employees. But first, they'd wait outside, giving Winn time to go up to the third floor using the elevator. Once there, she would take a "lookout" position not far from the stairs. When the coast was clear, she'd wave to Clay, and they'd hurry up the stairs and into their suite.

Winn arrived on the third floor and, with great stealth, stood near the stairwell keeping watch. A tall man stepped from the elevator, turned left, then walked down the hallway with his back to her. Pausing, he put his ear to her door and seemed to be listening. For what? Why? Had they left the TV on? She tried not to stare. This was not the time to call attention to herself. He looked slightly familiar, probably a hotel employee. Or was that the guy Clay had so fiercely removed from her room that first night in Denver? *That's ridiculous. Why would he still be around?*

Her thoughts derailed when she heard a light tap and a soft whine come from behind the door to the stairs. She turned toward her impatient partners and shook her head. Glancing down the hall again, Winn saw the man was gone, so she gave the all-clear wave. Clay dropped the leash, and the dog bounded down the hallway all the way to the end where it turned around and sat. Winn handed her bag to Clay and hurried after the dog. She gave him a pat on the head and picked up the leash.

"Let's go to your new home." *At least for a couple of days.* "Clay is waiting for us."

They'd arrived. All three were in and unscathed. Clay propped the door open between their two suites so the dog could freely dash back and forth. They turned both TVs on to muffle and disguise the pitter-pattering sound of dog paws that might travel down to the suites below them.

Instead of sticking to the evening's pre-planned activities, they stayed in to take care of the dog. Feeding him was a joyful experience. He ate the kibble as if he hadn't eaten in a long time. They laughed, watching him drink the water from the bowl. He dripped water on the floor, causing them to wonder where he learned to drink so sloppily.

When Clay asked Winn what she'd like to have for dinner, she replied, "Dinner could be tricky. We can't leave our new dog alone."

"It will be easy. You keep the dog in your suite, and I'll have our food delivered to mine. When the food arrives, I'll bring the cart over. How does that sound?"

"Perfect, just perfect. I'll have a steak, a baked potato, and a salad."

As Clay predicted, ordering the meal worked like a charm. Amazingly, the dog did not come close to them as they ate. He went into Winn's bedroom and watched them from the doorway with his head on his paws.

"I wonder if he's been abused,' Winn asked. "How else would he end up in the Last Chance cage?"

"I don't know," Clay said, "but he must have had good owners at some point in his life."

After Clay put the cart in the hall, they sat on the sofa, and the dog lay in front of them. How should they handle the next two days? How would it all play out? They also needed to name their dog. That task proved to be a challenge. They studied the black, floppy-eared dog hoping for inspiration. None came.

"What kind of dog do you think he is?" Having more experience with cats, she deferred to Clay.

"I definitely see some Lab in him, but his face reminds me of a Pit Bull." That information, though only a guess, didn't produce any names that suited the dog.

"I know that we're lucky to have found this wonderful dog. Maybe a great name will come to us tomorrow."

Clay nodded. "And he's lucky that we took a walk in the park today."

After a moment of silence, they looked at the dog and shouted, "Lucky!" That was the perfect name for their dog. Then, they prayed that their lucky dog was not a barker.

Chapter Five

December 17

Clay tossed and turned, his head swirling as he wondered about the consequences of suddenly becoming an escort with a dog. Would it cancel out his fantasy? Finally, an encouraging thought came to mind. How would they know he had a dog? They wouldn't. Ah. Sweet sleep soon arrived.

Awakened from a deep sleep by an unaccustomed sound, he jumped out of bed to find Lucky in the sitting area growling at a piece of paper by the door.

"It's okay, bud." After retrieving the scary paper from the floor, he scratched the dog's ears to calm him, checked his water dish, and returned to the bedroom. He glanced at the events scheduled for tomorrow—Tour of the Coors factory, a hockey game, ice-skating, and, if time allowed, the Denver Museum of Nature and

Science. He drifted to sleep, thinking about all the fun Winn would miss and feeling sorry for her.

With the addition of the dog, her city-life fantasy had become something else. What could he do to make it up to her? If only he had the power to control the weather. He knew a little snow would bring a smile to Winn's pretty face.

Clay didn't know if it was the sun streaming through the window and into his eyes or the soft growling coming from their furry friend again. Either way, he'd overslept, but suddenly he was fully awake. Looking into the sitting room, he was surprised to see the dog attending to another sheet of paper on the floor just inside the door.

"Hey, Lucky. What've you got there?"

Instead of an answer, the dog picked up the paper with its teeth and playfully shook it around like a squeaky toy. Clay grabbed it before it went through the canine shredder and was staring at the words on the page when Winn walked in.

With her head tilted, she asked, "Are you okay? You look like you've seen a ghost."

"Yeah, I'm okay. No ghosts here, but maybe a fortune teller or a mind reader. At the very least, a spy is lurking around."

"That sounds ominous. Tell me more. The suspense is killing me." She laughed, looking beautiful with her hair flowing loosely on her shoulders and wearing a silky blue nightgown.

"I've received an updated itinerary for today, and it's written as if someone from the Friendly Escort Service now knows we have a dog. Here. Take a look." He handed Winn the sheet of paper. She glanced at it, then handed it back.

"Well, what do you think of today's plan?"

She frowned and looked upward before speaking. "I think you are the escort. You're in charge. Our day is all up to you."

Clay shrugged, surprised that she'd go along with his employer's arrangements for the dog. Someone watched their every move and knew what they were doing even when they strayed from the itinerary. That did not sit well with him. Feelings of anger threatened to surface.

"We'd better get dressed. The limo will be here to pick up all three of us in forty-five minutes."

Winn was back in Clay's suite in ten minutes. She looked beautiful, but her choice of clothing was all-wrong for today's activities. He wasn't comfortable telling her what to wear, but he had to. "That's what you want to wear today?"

"Sure. Why not?"

"I thought you read the itinerary."

"Yes. I saw it."

Lacking the right words, he blurted out, "You need to change. You look pretty in that dress, and you know I like your hair like that, but right after the Coors Tour, we'll be going to a hockey game and then ice-skating on that same rink."

Her face turned bright orange. *Clothing is no big deal.* She quietly said, "Oh," and hurried back to her suite. She returned in three minutes wearing appropriate clothing. *That girl is fast.*

"Mr. Washington?" When Clay nodded, the limo driver opened the door for the three passengers. Inside, a breakfast of pastries, coffee, and juice awaited them. Dishes filled with water and dog food were secured in a box on the floor.

Opening the window that separated the driver from his passengers, the driver said, "Next stop, the Coors Factory. Sit back and relax. Should you require anything else, just press any of the silver buttons." He closed the window giving Clay, Winn, and Lucky some privacy.

When they arrived at the enormous factory's entrance, the driver assured them that he would take excellent care of the dog and be back in two hours to pick them up. Clay and Winn looked each other in the eye, then turned toward Lucky, who smiled and wagged his tail. He appeared completely happy as he hopped back into the limo. They waved goodbye to their lucky dog and began their tour.

Winn seemed fascinated by the pre-recorded audio tour explaining the brewing process. At the end of the tour, they were led into The Tasting Room. "Do you think they will let me have a little taste? I saw a young woman in the line ahead of us, showing her ID. I didn't bring mine, and even if I had, it would show I'm only twenty."

Winn breathed a sigh of relief when no one requested to see her ID. They each tasted three free samples. The glasses were small and held a safe amount of beer, even for a non-drinker like Winn. Clay took great pleasure in observing her enthusiasm over the tour and the three drinks.

"I never knew there were so many varieties of beer." She asked if she could try a few more. Clay stepped to the counter to fulfill her request and returned with samples bearing fruity names, some containing the word *cider*. They continued sipping for another twenty minutes.

Clay checked his watch. It was time to go. When he stood, Winn followed his lead but lost her balance and nearly fell. He grabbed her by the arm to give support.

"I'm fine. I don't need any help. I just got up too fast," she insisted, feeling woozy.

"Yes, ma'am. Whatever you say." He motioned with his arm for her to go ahead of him. "Ladies first."

She curtsied like the bell of the ball before heading to the floor again. Clay was ready. He caught her around the waist with both arms and held her tightly, lifting her to a standing position.

A brewery employee was at their side in a flash. "Is there a problem here?"

Clay answered immediately. "No, sir. She just gets

vertigo sometimes. We're fine, but thanks for your concern."

Turning, body-to-body and face-to-face, their eyes met and carried new meaning this time. The look was not about a bad-intentioned stranger or a Last Chance dog. It was all about them. Neither spoke, but Clay felt something that he, as her *friendly escort*, should not feel and did not want to feel.

He had plans of his own, and they didn't include a woman, at least not for a while. He wondered what she felt standing here with his arms around her. Her gaze up at him looked sweet and dreamy . . . but that could be the beer.

Back in the limo, Lucky welcomed them with dog kisses and tail wags. The driver handed them cups of coffee. Winn spoke very little but sat extremely close to Clay on the ride to the Pepsi Center arena to watch the Colorado Avalanche hockey team play. At the end of the game, two players escorted Winn and Clay down to the ice and outfitted them with skates. The players, in full uniform, laughed as they asked, "Do you want any sticks or pucks?"

"No, thanks." The act of skating would be challenging enough for both of them. Clay had a slight advantage, having skated a few times earlier in his life.

The arena lights dimmed, and music played as the two skated slowly, cautiously around the rink, holding hands. The blades of their skates connected a few times, tripping them and giving them an up-close-and-personal view of the ice. They laughed and had a great time, even though a few sore muscles and bruises would likely show up on their bodies tomorrow.

Pulling up to the hotel entrance, the driver said, "Ms. Wahlberg, I'll be here tomorrow to take you to the airport."

Winn and Clay exchanged downcast looks until an idea came to mind. "You know, she won't need a ride. I'm renting a car tomorrow, and I'll be happy to take her." Turning toward Winn, he added, "If that's okay with you."

She threw her arms around him. "That is better than okay. It's magnificent and thoughtful. Thank you." She kissed him on the cheek. He kissed her back on the lips.

Chapter Six

December 18

Well-rested and happy, Winn and Lucky bounded into Clay's suite. Ever since the dog arrived and they'd kept the adjoining door open, they thought of their living arrangement as one large suite with two bedrooms. Actually, two of everything.

"What are we doing today?" she asked, giving the dog a pat. She sat on the floor with the dog's head in her lap. Both looked up, waiting for Clay's answer.

Instead of saying anything, he went to the door, opened it, and looked out into the hallway. First toward the floor, then left and right. He scratched his head and said, "I don't know. There's no itinerary. I had strict instructions to follow each day's itinerary."

"Oh, Clay. You know very well we've strayed from

doing that. Maybe, since we were so good at *straying*, we've been given a free day to do whatever we want."

"Yeah. That does make sense. You've got your plane ticket, right? What time does your flight take off?"

Happiness took a backseat to a feeling of melancholy. "I was trying not to think about leaving, but I know my city-girl week is almost over. I'm all packed. All I need to do is drop my keycard off at the desk."

She told him her flight left at 5:20 p.m., and she was supposed to arrive two hours before that.

"Great. We have enough time to make your last day your best day. Do you think you can handle walking Lucky by yourself?" Winn nodded, her arms wrapped around the dog. "Good. When you return from your walk, order breakfast from Room Service. I'll be back in a jiffy. Got some business to take care of." He gave the dog's ears a scratch and Winn's forehead a kiss.

"Are you kissing me because it's a job requirement?" She batted her eyelashes, something she never would have done a week ago.

"No. Romantic or physical gestures were not part of my contract. However, by the end of your city-gal fantasy, the Friendly Escort Service will want to know that you're a happy camper."

"Interesting. A happy camper in the city. That's a bit ironic, don't you think?"

Clay shrugged and hurried out the door.

"Come on, Lucky. Let's take our morning walk." Slight pangs of apprehension traveled through her body, remembering the last time she walked this hallway alone. She'd be cautious, vigilant. Apparently, Lucky felt her tension because as she opened the door to the suite, the dog stopped and looked up and down the hallway before stepping out. "We're quite a team," she laughed, trying to squash the sadness that lingered in her heart.

Clay returned, jingling car keys, as a broad smile spread across his face. "Got a 4WD Jeep, a scenic drive loaded into my GPS, and the name of a highly recommended restaurant where we'll stop for a late lunch. Winn turned in her keycard at the desk while Clay loaded her bags and Lucky into the Jeep.

Holding hands, neither spoke. Clay wasn't a man of many words; he was more of an action guy. And now he had mixed feelings about his feelings. This was not the right time to be distracted from his personal goals by a woman. He had to stick with his plans. He'd say good-bye and make sure she boarded the plane safely. Yes, he'd miss her, but he'd survive.

The drive was beautiful. Seeing snow at the top of the Rocky Mountains thrilled Winn, and the restaurant lived up to its rustic reputation. During their final course, warm country cobbler à la mode, Clay took out a box wrapped in holiday colors from his coat pocket and handed it to Winn.

"What's this?"

He thought about his answer. "It's a present to say goodbye and Happy early Birthday. Go on. Open it."

Anxious to see her reaction, he watched as she carefully unwrapped the bright, shiny package. What followed were tears and sighs.

"What's the matter? Did I do something wrong?"

"No. You did something right. Very right and kind. How did you know that I love and collect snow globes?"

When he answered, "I got lucky," they both laughed. "And, I thought since you didn't get your fantasy wish for snow, I'd deliver some."

The snow globe contained a man, a woman, and a dog. The snow fell on all three every time she shook it, and she shook it many times on the drive to the airport.

Clay parked the Jeep. From the back of the vehicle, he removed Winn's old yellow suitcase and the new one that held her expanded wardrobe.

Winn gave him a long and loving embrace and then hugged Lucky. "I'll see you again someday. In the meantime, Clay will take good care of you." The inevitable had arrived, and Clay fought against his conflicting feelings.

The airport was much larger and busier than Clay anticipated. He was darn glad he wasn't the one boarding a plane. He carried the yellow bag in one hand and pulled the new one with the other. Winn hooked her arm with his as they made their way toward the United counter to check-in.

There were long lines of holiday travelers waiting to get their boarding passes, check luggage, and go through security. "Good afternoon, Ms. Wahlberg. You're checking two bags today?" The woman behind the counter looked fatigued but managed a friendly tone and a weak smile. The smile faded when she looked at Winn's ticket. "I'm afraid we've got a problem."

Winn showed the woman her itinerary. "See. It says I depart today."

"Yes, ma'am. It does. But you missed your flight."

Clay entered the conversation. "I thought her flight left at 5:20 p.m. It's only 3:30."

"No, sir." She showed him the ticket. "United Flight 2744 departed at 2:50 p.m."

The expression on Winn's face was pure shock. A look of embarrassment soon followed. Confused by her reaction and the troubling situation, Clay put his arm around her. "Don't worry. We'll figure something out."

When Clay asked the woman to check for the next available flight, he learned the Yuma flights were solidly booked until after Christmas. They could get her to Phoenix the next day, but she would need to take a Greyhound bus to Yuma. Other travelers mumbled impatiently behind them, so Clay took her bags, and they walked away.

"I'm sorry to have made such a stupid mistake and caused so much trouble. What do you think I should do?"

This unfortunate situation gave Clay an idea. He

should probably give Fate or Cupid or The Fantasy Maker credit for the situation, but the idea, the new plan, was all his. He admitted to himself that he wanted to spend more time with Winn. Now, if only she'd go along with his plan. A plan that was too new to be fully formed.

Clay cashed in his own ticket that would have taken him to Montrose, Colorado, late the next day. "Let's take your bags back to the Jeep and return to the hotel. We can stay in my suite tonight. I don't have to check out till tomorrow."

"All right, but that doesn't get me home."

"I promise to get you home safely. Just know, it will take a little longer than the original plan."

He kissed her lips and pushed a tendril of hair from her eyes. She kissed him back, slowly, passionately. Her previous looks of shock and embarrassment were gone, replaced by a sweet look of — he couldn't say the word. He'd never said it before. He'd never felt it before. Did she feel the same way he did? Her eyes, the way they sparkled up into his, tugged at his heart. Oh, hell. Was she in love? Was he in love? Maybe this was pre-love or deep like or . . . *Stop thinking! Just shut up and drive.*

❄

They didn't try to hide the dog. The three of them walked in through the hotel's main entrance to the elevators as if they owned the place.

Winn knew her fantasy officially ended at 2:50 p.m. when her flight took off without her. Did the Friendly Escort Service or The Fantasy Maker know about this new situation? Somehow, one or the other had learned about the dog immediately.

Clay's job as her escort was over too. Surely, he had other work or family to attend to. Hadn't he mentioned something about checking out tomorrow and going to another Colorado location? What was his plan for her? She was dying to know.

Clay removed two soda cans from the mini-bar, opened them, and handed one to her. They sat on the sofa enjoying the view of the mountains in the distance. Still no clouds in the sky. No snow would fall tonight. Only half of her fantasy had come true. She hid her disappointment and silently scolded herself for not appreciating the wonderful week she'd been given.

Winn's curiosity inspired her to ask about his plan. "Come on, Clay. What gives? What's this spontaneous idea of yours?"

His eyes teased, his mouth grinned. "Curious, huh? You know what they say about the cat, right?"

"Sure. Doesn't everybody?" Then she scooted onto his lap, her thighs straddling his. Long wavy strands of her hair brushed against his neck. She held his face in her manicured hands. "Your plan better be good." Then she kissed him.

"What happened to the shy, small town girl with the tight ponytail?"

She tickled his ear with her tongue and whispered, "She's right here. And you, Mr. Washington, had better start talking."

By now, Lucky had jumped up on the sofa and joined the conversation. They had no idea what his woofs and whimpers meant, but he seemed to be having fun.

Clay began. "You're going to like what I'm about to say, and I'll even bet there will be snow involved." He had her full attention. He explained that he'd be helping out and learning about horses at a special ranch not far from Telluride, Colorado, and he invited her to go with him. "What do you say?"

Her eyes opened wide with excitement. She would go anywhere with Clay. She could take more time off work, but losing another week of pay was a problem. There would be costs involved in this extra jaunt to a horse ranch. She stalled, not knowing what to say.

"Why are you hesitating? Do you have a better idea?"

She saw the anticipation in his eyes and wished she had a better answer. "I can't afford another vacation."

"This won't cost you a penny. Once we're there, we'll be staying in a cabin stocked with plenty of food and drink supplied by none other than The Fantasy Maker."

"What did you just say?" Her good feelings faded. Less naïve than she was five days ago, she knew something was off. "My special vacation is over. Why would The Fantasy Maker do that?"

Clay appeared to be thinking about his answer. "Yeah. I wanted to tell you about my own fantasy, but I wasn't allowed to while I was your escort."

"So you've been lying to me from the moment we met?"

"I never lied to you. You assumed I lived in Denver. The contract I had with The Fantasy Maker didn't allow me to tell you the terms of my agreement. I applied for a fantasy just like you did. I was given one, but with strings and conditions attached. I agreed to work for The Friendly Escort Service for five days to earn my fantasy."

"You're not really a city guy, are you?"

"Nope. I'm a Kansas farm boy who went off to college against his parents' wishes. They needed me on the farm, but when Dad added raising poultry to our wheat business, I couldn't deal with that. Those chickens were the last straw."

"Let me summarize the situation." She felt the heat rising on her face and anger about to boil over in her gut. "You left your family in a lurch and got yourself a cool fantasy vacation by lying to me and pretending to be someone you are not." Her arms crossed tightly against her breasts as she puffed out an infuriated breath.

At the end of her tirade, she turned away from his glare and ran to the adjoining door only to find it locked. She sank to the floor feeling like the oxygen had been knocked from her lungs. Wanting to hide, she covered her face with her hands. The dog ran over to her and showered her with kisses. Clay came next, took her hand, and led her to the bedroom. Was this where they'd kiss and make up? Was that what she wanted?

"The room is all yours. I'll sleep on the couch." He spoke without emotion, his tone as cold as ice. He left her alone, closing the door behind him.

Winn sat on the edge of Clay's bed, staring out the window. Her tears blurred the beautiful view of the foothills. She laid back and closed her eyes hoping sleep would relieve her of the misery she felt. Instead of falling asleep, a lengthy list of pros and cons concerning Clay and The Fantasy Maker kept her awake.

Clay was a good-natured and good-looking man, but from the beginning, she had concerns about his occasional fits of anger that rose up suddenly. He'd been kind and thoughtful and made her body tingle with womanly feelings, but darn, this wonderful man had lied to her and misrepresented himself. He was an imposter. Her sleep-denying thoughts turned to The Fantasy Maker. Winter knew nothing about this person. Or was it an organization? A flash of fear surged through her veins realizing that she hadn't enough information to generate any accurate pros or cons.

Far beyond the boundaries of her comfort zone and frustrated with herself, she threw one of the bed pillows over her face to hide from the world. She managed to block out the universe, but not Clay. The pillow carried the tantalizing scent of his cologne, reminding her of his whispers into her ear and his strong arms holding her, providing comfort and safety.

When a vision of him speaking sweetly to Lucky and to the squirrels and birds in the park came to mind, tears welled up. She rolled onto her side and hugged the pillow as if her life, her existence, depended on this inanimate object. She should never have let herself fall for this man. What had her mother said on several occasions? "Even if a man appears to be a perfect, cool drink of water, remember, hon, you are NOT thirsty."

Those words of warning kept repeating in her head like a scratchy, broken record. She didn't hear the knock on the door, but she felt Clay's deliciously-scented body snuggled up behind her.

"I'm sorry," he whispered. "I'm not a perfect man. Can we start over?"

She turned to face him. Choking back her convulsive sobs, she gently stroked his cheek. "I'm the one who should apologize. If I'd read my plane ticket correctly, I'd be out of your hair by now, and you could get on with your life."

"The plane ticket mix-up was odd, but I'm glad it happened."

"Really?" A sliver of happiness edged into her heart. Should she explain the mix-up? She knew exactly how it happened.

"I don't know where I'll be after my fantasy comes to an end. I should go back to my family's farm and help them grow wheat and raise chickens, but I'd rather have my own small ranch and raise hay for a few therapy horses."

Clay reached for the phone and ordered a light dinner from room service. They moved back to the sitting area to be with Lucky and watch the moon rise while they waited for their food to arrive. He held her hand and told her how relieved he was to stop pretending to be a street-wise city guy. He apologized again for having misled her. "Now I have a new problem. You seemed to like that city guy. I am not that guy. And, just so you know, my real wardrobe consists of jeans and T-shirts, baseball caps, and cowboy hats."

His comment made her laugh. "But you're keeping the new clothes, right?"

"I suppose so. They might come in handy someday."

Winn nodded and then, with careful consideration, decided that she had a fact or two to share. "I've never lied to you, Clay, though I may have omitted a few things about myself. But I did lie to my parents about this trip. They never would have let me out of the house if they knew the truth."

"What lie did you tell them?"

"I told them I was attending a Caregiver Conference in Denver, and it was required for my pending promotion at the nursing home."

"Wow! That's a whopper!" He grinned and wiggled his eyebrows up and down.

"You're happy that I lied to my parents?" she asked, with a hint of skepticism.

He leaned closer and gave her bottom lip a gentle nibble. "Yep. I wouldn't want you to be perfect. Now we have something in common."

"Do I want to know what that is?"

"Of course. We're both imperfect and have some parental issues."

She pulled back sharply, and panic took over her senses. "My parents are expecting my phone call to let them know that I've arrived at the Yuma Airport. My call is overdue. They are either worried sick or madder than wet hens."

"I'd rather there was no mention of poultry." A mischievous grin accompanied his comment.

Clay helped her think of a solution to this sudden, problematic detail. They made up a story—another whopper. Clay wrote down what she would say to her parents. *Hi, Mom. Guess what? I did so well at the conference that they asked me to stay for part two of the training. There would be hands-on workshops at various nursing homes and hospitals in the Denver area. So, I'll be home in about a week. Love you.* "Now, go make that call."

Winn held the paper in one hand as she dialed the number with the other, but she never even glanced at it when speaking to her mother. There was no point. She couldn't read the words fast enough but managed to deliver an adequate version of the message.

"Bye, Mom."

"Don't keep me in suspense. What did she say?"

"She's happy that I'm doing so well, and she wished me luck. I feel so guilty."

"Yeah. That makes two of us."

Their thoughts diverted when they heard unidentifiable noises coming from the hallway. Lucky growled and moved toward the door. Clay and Winn looked at each other. Before either reached the door's peephole, they heard "Room Service" and breathed a sigh of relief. The noise was dinner arriving.

Remembering what Lala had said about the dog's temperament, Clay held onto Lucky while Winn opened the door to receive the dinner cart from the hotel employee. There stood a man wearing one of the hotel's Room Service jackets, but a surgical-type mask covered most of his face.

Clay called out over the dog's insistent barking, "Hey, man. Are you sick?"

The man shook his head. "Just allergies." Then walked away without getting Clay's signature on the dinner ticket. They distracted the upset dog with a few bites of people food, and he settled down.

"He looked familiar," Winn commented. "And Lucky did not like him."

"It was probably the mask. I've known dogs to freak out seeing a man wearing a cowboy hat. Let's eat up before our food gets cold."

After dinner, the tables turned. Winn took Clay's

hand and led him into the bedroom. "Please sleep with me tonight." She needed the closeness.

The humans curled up together like flexible spoons.

The dog stretched out at the foot of the king-sized bed.

All was well in Suite 305.

Chapter Seven

December 19

Clay watched Winn walk to the window and slide open the heavy curtain. By the dim light of dawn, he saw this was not going to be a snow day. The temperature cooperated, but the cloudless sky made any precipitation unlikely.

"No clouds," she murmured as if speaking to herself.

If only he could make it snow, her fantasy would be complete. *I don't have that kind of power.* Or did he? He had an idea. Jumping into his jeans and pulling a long-sleeve T-shirt over his head, he dashed toward the door.

"I'll be right back. Just going to the lobby for a second."

Winn showered and was bent over towel-drying her hair, wearing next to nothing, when Clay returned.

"You're moving rapidly this morning," she said, not looking up. "Do I need to hurry?"

"No. Drying your hair is a good idea, though. It's going to be very cold today." Luckily, with all her hair falling over her face, she didn't see the bag Clay slipped into his rolling suitcase.

The 4WD Jeep Cherokee was tightly packed, leaving just enough room for Lucky on one side of the back seat. They'd each arrived in Denver with one bag, but now they each had two to accommodate their new city duds. Clay used the *maps* feature on his phone to obtain driving directions to guide them from downtown Denver to Telluride. The drive would take approximately six hours. They'd arrive in time for a late lunch.

They made several stops to stretch their legs and let Lucky do his business. To their enjoyment, Lucky was amazing and smart. They speculated about his prior experiences and how he ended up in the Last Chance crate. He seemed happy and well adjusted in their company, and that's all that mattered.

Now and then, Clayed slowed down, looked in his rearview mirror, and then sped up. "What are you doing? Is something wrong with the Jeep?"

"No, I'm just checking on the car behind us. Nothing to worry about."

"I'm not worried, but I am curious." She smiled and

placed her hand on his thigh. "A little more information, please."

Did he want to share his hunch about the car behind them? No, not really. His words came out slowly. "I think the car might be following us. Whenever I slow down, it slows down. When I speed up, it seems to speed up too. No big deal. It's probably nothing."

"I'm sure it's nothing," Winn added, grinning. "Maybe the driver is a woman, and she's stalking you because you're so good-looking."

Clay took her teasing as a good sign. A sign she wasn't worried. Subtly, he kept his eye on the car behind them. Who'd bother to stalk him? What a ridiculous thought.

They arrived in the quaint mountain town of Telluride before two o'clock. They parked the Jeep and cracked open all the windows so Lucky would have fresh air without getting too cold.

"We'll be back as soon as we get some lunch," he told the dog.

Holding gloved hands, they walked up and down Colorado Avenue glancing at the colorful Christmas decorations in the windows of the shops and restaurants. The town was devoid of snow, which bothered Clay. He'd taken this slight detour certain snow would cover the ground, the streets, everything. Fortunately, he noticed that the mountain peaks surrounding them were covered with plenty of the white stuff.

"Well, it's our lucky day." Pointing upward, he added, "There's your snow."

"Nope. It's so far away that I might as well be looking at a picture on a postcard. I would love to see snow falling from the sky, landing on my nose and on my tongue. I want to see if snow really crunches when I step on it." Winn laughed loudly. "And, I want to throw a snowball at you."

He was too hungry and cold to think of a clever comment. "Let's stop at the next restaurant we come to, no matter what kind of food it serves." The next restaurant was The Brown Dog. How appropriate. The Brown Dog was warm, rustic, and filled with joyful people. Winn and Clay shared a pizza before hurrying back to check on their black dog.

When they reached the Jeep, it was only 3:45 p.m., but the sun had dipped behind the high mountain peaks, and the temperature dropped. They would no longer leave Lucky in the car alone. With the heater running full blast, Clay made some calls on his cell phone to acquire accommodations for the night. Many hotels were pet-friendly, but the town was fully booked because Christmas was only a few days away.

He turned toward Winn and shrugged. "I'm on hold. The woman at the Telluride Reservation Center had to take another call."

"Mr. Washington, you're in luck. We just had a cancelation at the Lost Creek Inn. Do you know where that is?"

"No, ma'am. This is our first time in Telluride."

"Find Oak Street and head downhill. At the bottom of that hill, you'll find transportation to Mountain Village, where your hotel is located. Have a wonderful time."

They high-fived each other, noticing their dog held up his paw. Really? This dog from the Last Chance crate does tricks? Must be a coincidence? After their palms connected with his paw, they threw a few items of clothing into a duffle bag Clay had in the car, attached the leash to Lucky's collar, and headed off in search of Oak Street, which was only three short blocks away.

Looking around and not seeing any form of transportation, Winn asked a warmly-dressed woman walking a dog where they'd find a ride to Mountain Village. She merely pointed and said, "Over there," and kept on walking.

They both looked in the direction of the woman's gesture. Clay's eyes glazed over as he stared up, way up. Winn jumped for joy. "Wow! A gondola! Look, Clay. I think it goes all the way up to the snow. This is so wonderful, so perfect. I've never been on one, have you?" She didn't wait for his answer but took off running to the gondola boarding area holding Lucky by his leash.

Clay loved seeing her so happy and wished he could share her enthusiasm. He caught up to where she waited in line and suggested they find another way to the hotel. When the next pet-friendly gondola swung around, the attendant motioned for the three of them to hop on. Lucky went first, Winn second. The door closed, and Clay was not with them. He stood with his hands in his pockets, watching them head up the steep hill. The gondola swayed in the wind, and two faces, one shocked, the other obliviously happy, stared down at him.

He felt like a jerk, a gutless failure.

If the view was magnificent, Winn missed it, her sight blurred by the tears filling her eyes. How could he let her ride up the mountain without him? Would he join her later, or had he abandoned her? She recalled he'd acted strangely during part of the drive today.

Unable to make sense of this distressing situation, she did the only thing she could think of. She wiped away the tears from her cheeks before the gondola slowed down and the door opened. They exited and Winn began looking for the Lost Creek Inn. She spotted it quickly, but Lucky wanted no part of walking down the long flight of metal, grid-like snow stairs. She didn't want to force him and hoped to find an alternate way down.

A slender woman with a toddler in a snowsuit stopped to ask if they could pet the dog.

"This is Lucky. He's a rescue dog and I've only

known him for a few days. I'm not certain how he'll behave around children."

"I understand." She gave the dog a quizzical look. "He doesn't want to use those scary stairs, huh? Follow me. I know another way." The woman led Winn and Lucky around the corner to an elevator.

"Thank you," Winn called out as the elevator closed.

Most of the walkways around Mountain Village were without snow, but the ski slopes were bright white. A man selling hot chocolate near a colorfully-painted, old-fashioned phone booth, explained that this was a bad year for snow and machines made just enough of the white stuff to keep a few of the runs open. Sipping the hot drink she'd purchased, Winn and the dog headed to the hotel.

Lucky growled and pulled on his leash. Something or someone had upset him. She hadn't seen him act like this since the hotel worker with allergies had delivered their dinner one night. "Come on, Lucky. We're almost at the hotel. You're going to be fine. You'll see."

They entered the lobby of the Lost Creek Inn. Winn searched with her eyes, Lucky with his nose, but they both came up empty. Clay was not there.

A young man at the front desk said, "Welcome to the Inn. Can I help you?"

"Yes. We have a reservation under the name Clay Washington."

"Ah, yes, you do." He showed her where the room

was located on the map and handed her the keycard and a leaflet. "Here's information about our rules and amenities for pets. Enjoy your stay."

She had to stay the night; she had nowhere else to go. Moving slowly to the room, uncertain about her immediate future, she slipped the keycard into the slot. Lucky wiggled and whined and vaulted into the room the second the door opened.

"Clay!"

"Hi, Winn." He helped her out of her winter coat before hugging the exuberant dog. "We need to talk."

He looked intently into her eyes, but all she saw was his injured right fist. "What happened? Your hand is scraped and bloody." Before he had time to respond, she shouted, "Were you fighting again?" Clay's propensity to save people in peril or settle differences with physical violence made her uncomfortable.

"Yeah, but I was fighting with . . ."

"I want to be with you," she interrupted, "but I think I should go home. To be honest, sometimes you scare me." She sank down into the over-stuffed chair that faced the window and felt empty inside. She had nothing more to say.

"Would it help to know that I was fighting with myself?"

Stunned, she stammered, "You punched yourself? That's crazy."

"No, I punched a tree. I was angry with myself for keeping one more small piece of information from you."

She cocked her head. "I'm listening."

He paced for several minutes in front of the large window, the dog's head following his every move as if he were watching the ball in a tennis match. Clay finally sat and seemed ready to talk, his leg bouncing up and down like a four-year-old who needed to use the bathroom. Looking sheepish, he blurted out, "I don't do well with heights. I don't ride up steep mountains dangling from a gondola."

Winn snuggled up on his lap and wrapped her arms around him. "I think I understand."

He nodded and ran his fingers through her beautiful, wavy hair. "I'd like another do-over."

"Are there limits to those?"

"Not that I'm aware of."

"That's good." Winn had one more question. How did Clay get here if he didn't ride the gondola? He explained there was a paved road between Telluride and Mountain Village. He'd gone back to get the Jeep and drove quickly, hoping to arrive before she did. Satisfied with his explanation, she said, "I think it's time we kissed and made up."

One kiss turned into two, three, and four. They'd likely still be kissing if Lucky hadn't scratched on the door with his paw. Knowing what that meant, they slipped into their warm clothing and strolled through the town of Mountain Village, taking in the vast views of majestic snow-covered peaks and picturesque valleys off in the distance. The architecture was amazing, like nothing either of them had ever seen. There were private homes as large as hotels decorated with moving reindeer, smiling Santas, and awesome light shows.

Amid shops and eating establishments, they came upon a pet-grooming boutique where they purchased a coat for Lucky and a doggie bag with two days' worth of kibble. The larger container of dog food was in the Jeep.

After gleefully ordering delicious-smelling Italian food To Go, they walked back to the Inn. All three ate ravenously before climbing into the king-sized bed to snuggle and watch TV. Clay and Lucky fell asleep before ten minutes passed. Watching them sleep so peacefully brought a smile to her face, but her mind swirled with a troubling dilemma.

Tomorrow morning they'd drive to the horse rescue and therapy ranch where Clay's fantasy would take place. She wanted to be honest with him but didn't want anything to spoil his chance to experience his dream of working with abused or abandoned horses. Should she confess her own fears and secrets and risk damaging their budding relationship?

❄

"What do you mean you don't know where they are? Winn should be back in Yuma by now, and Clay should be at the ranch south of Telluride. What the hell happened?"

"When I said I'd be back to drive Winn to the

airport, she declined the offer. Actually, *they* declined the offer. It wasn't the right time to explain who I was, and I'm sure Clay wanted to take her. I saw no problem with that."

"How do you know Winn is not in Yuma?"

"I assumed she was, but when I discovered Clay hadn't arrived at the ranch, I decided to investigate both of their whereabouts. An old friend of mine was able to take a look at the passenger lists. Winn wasn't on the plane to Yuma, and Clay wasn't on the plane to Montrose."

"How could you have let this happen? Damn it, Martin. Find her. I'm okay with the fact that Clay hasn't arrived yet. His official fantasy doesn't begin until tomorrow, and he can take care himself. Track her down first."

Martin knew that mistakes had been made, but several strange and unplanned events had occurred, complicating his job this time. The Fantasy Maker was also partly to blame. This problem wouldn't exist if they'd stuck with the original plan to keep all the fantasies closer to one of the coastlines. That made it possible for The Fantasy Maker to assist in monitoring the fantasy recipient's activities. That was the plan he'd agreed to. Covertly overseeing two fantasies at once with the brains of the company many land and nautical miles away, was not.

"What's your next move, Martin?"

"I'll get back to you on that."

Chapter Eight

December 20

Clay couldn't contain his excitement. He'd spent most of his life on a farm, but finally, he'd spend a week on a horse ranch learning about rehabilitating neglected or abused horses, healing their wounds inside and out. He wanted to take an active part in giving the horses a fresh start, a chance at a good life.

Winn pointed at the rustic, wooden speed limit sign wrapped in a holiday garland. Ahead, barns, corrals, and cabins came into view. Several horses grazed calmly in a distant pasture. As they drove closer, they observed other horses pacing in their round pens.

"Uh, Clay? You're speeding." She smiled at the man sitting beside her, acting more like a small boy on Christmas morning racing for the gifts under the tree.

He nodded. "Thanks. I don't want to start off on the wrong foot with the owners of the ranch."

"Do you know the owners?"

"No. I'm supposed to seek out a lady named Margie. Maybe that's her over there."

A woman wearing a baseball cap looked up from assisting a farrier trimming a horse's hoof. She waved them over. "Hi. I'm Margie. You must be Clay Washington. Welcome to the ranch." Margie's eyes focused on the person in the passenger seat. "I see you've brought a friend."

Clay hoped that wouldn't be a problem, and, from the look on Winn's face, she had a similar thought.

Winn jumped from the Jeep, stepped over to Margie, and held out her hand. "My name is Winn Wahlberg. I missed my flight in Denver, and Clay was kind enough to let me tag along with him for a day or two. I can stay inside the cabin. I promise I won't be in the way."

"Well, Ms. Wahlberg, today you can be a guest. Tomorrow, I'm putting you to work."

Clay jumped in, saying, "I'm ready to work right now." He didn't want to waste a single minute of his ranch time.

Margie insisted they unpack and get settled in their assigned cabin. Then said, "Fire up the woodstove because the next few days will be extremely cold." They put their suitcases and the dog's items in the cabin. It was a small, one-room dwelling, constructed to look very old and rustic. Still, it had enough modern conveniences.

A tour of the facility was first on the day's agenda. "Let's take the tour," Clay said, even though they had not unpacked. Anxious to get on with his fantasy, he clipped the leash to the dog's collar, grabbed Winn's hand, and they dashed out the door.

"Hold it right there, cowboy. I'm afraid some of these horses are not ready to meet an unfamiliar animal. Sorry, but the dog needs to stay in your cabin."

Clay started to speak up. "He's a newly rescued dog . . ."

Margie interrupted his explanation. "All the more reason to leave him behind."

Winn made a decision. "No problem. I'll stay with him in the cabin. Enjoy your tour. Come on, Lucky."

Margie tossed a pair of leather gloves to Clay. "Do you ride?"

Her question caught him off guard. Did he need to ride horses? Would his lack of riding experience be an issue? "I grew up on a farm and rode tractors and simple combines most of the time." He avoided answering her question but at least hadn't lied.

Margie smiled, "We'll start from the ground up, but you will get on one of my gentle therapy horses before you leave. That's not negotiable."

The landscape, the buildings, and especially the eight rescued horses were magnificent. Clay was surprised to hear that Margie had therapy horses too that helped adults and children with physical and mental health challenges.

After the first part of the tour, Clay, the rookie cowboy, stood by the Jeep with Margie, the master horsewoman, for a bit of Q & A. He had a million questions regarding the horses' limitations as well as their talents, but his first questions screeched to a halt when he heard a troubling sound coming from the cabin. He knew that sound. It was Lucky snarling, barking, and growling louder than ever before.

Margie shook her head, then shrugged. "Go!"

He took off running. Winn and Lucky needed him.

※

Lucky stood stiffly on his hind legs looking out the side window, still barking when Clay burst through the door. This was nothing like his I-see-a-squirrel bark. It was more an If-you-dare-enter-this-cabin-I-will-hurt-you bark.

"What happened? Why is he so upset?"

"I don't know. Lucky must have seen or heard something he deemed dangerous."

Clay scratched his head, his frustration obvious. "Deemed dangerous? Really? Dogs don't deem."

"This is not the time to quibble over my vocabulary. Something frightened him, which in turn frightened me. We should trust the dog."

Clay went to the window. "All that's out there is a

thick grove of Aspen trees. They look harmless to me."
His voice carried a tone of sarcasm.

"Well, aren't you astute."

"See? See what I mean? Can't you just use plain,
everyday words?" A knock at the door put a hold on
their bickering. "You've got a dictionary, right?" She
nodded. "Get it out. I'm going to need it because this
discussion isn't over."

"Hey, you two. Is everything all right?"

"Come on in, Margie. We're fine now. It seems a
grove of trees scared the dog."

Winn glared at Clay. How could he be so unsympa-
thetic? No, that was too kind of a word. He was rude
and lacked empathy. She'd seen him angry before, but
there'd always been a logical reason for his expression of
annoyance. This was different. This was inexplicably
appalling. Feeling a touch spiteful, she unpacked her
dictionary and placed it on the small table.

Turning her attention to the dog, Margie spoke
softly and rubbed him gently. The frightening event was
over. "Winn, why don't you stay up at the main house
while Clay and I finish the tour. The cook and my business manager are there, so you won't be alone."

"Thank you. That would be nice." She put a few
dog treats in her coat pocket and reached for the leash.

"I'm sorry. He can't come with you. Only service
dogs are allowed in the buildings at the ranch. If I made
an exception for you, there'd be no end to the requests of
others."

"That's all right. I understand. We'll be fine right here." She watched Clay and Margie walk away as if nothing unusual had happened.

She didn't want to be alone, but she refused to leave Lucky by himself so soon after his ferocious outburst. Maybe their dog did have a few deep-seated problems. They could work with him, help him, if necessary. But was Clay's change in attitude and sudden outburst fixable? He was far from trouble-free. He proved that today. Could she handle two rescue dogs? Did she want to?

❄

December 21

Clay rolled over and groaned. His body ached like never before. After the tour ended, Margie had put him to work. He'd lifted bales of hay and alfalfa, mucked stalls, filled water troughs, exercised one of the kid-friendly therapy horses in the round pen, and assisted the farrier as he trimmed two horses' hooves. He loved every minute of it. The activity chased away his grumpy mood, but some of his muscles, those that had lain dormant for a while, were whining loudly.

Winn sat up and asked, "Do you realize you are groaning and smiling simultaneously? Or is that a grimace?"

He rolled over again. This time, he pulled her up on

top of him and held her tightly. "What's a grimace?" Yesterday, her words were his enemy. This morning, words were funny. He managed to stifle his laughter.

"It's the smile of a Grinch." They both laughed. That laughter led to kissing. The kissing led to Lucky jumping up on the bed to join the fun. "He's doing fine today. After I take him for a long, leash walk, I think I'll come out and watch you and the horses for a while."

"I would love that. I don't know what I'm doing yet, but Margie said I was a natural around the horses. I want to turn this fantasy into reality someday." He'd never be the owner of a ranch like this—*that would be a fantasy*—but he could be a ranch hand or even a ranch manager.

He dressed quickly, gulped down the coffee Winn made, and put on his warm barn coat, gloves, and cowboy hat before heading out. "I think we should go to bed early tonight." His parting words were followed by a persuasive wink.

Day Two of his fantasy was about to begin. He found Margie in the main barn turning out some of the horses to the pasture and others to their outdoor stalls. He learned that he wouldn't be feeding and mucking today. Instead, he had a full day of hands-on horse work ahead of him.

Winn didn't often have warm, fuzzy feelings for her mother, but the past two days changed all that. She found a new appreciation for her mother's ability to cook delicious meals and cope with the fluctuating moods of a man. Having never done either, she'd taken those talents for granted. Now, as she stood staring into the fridge, she wished she'd paid more attention when her mother was busy in the kitchen.

Last night's dinner was easy to fix. She simply read the directions on the back of a frozen lasagna package and popped it in the oven. Clay had been hungry, and that satisfied him. For tonight, she found no pre-made dinners. She needed to put ingredients together to create a meal. Clay's parting words this morning inspired her to create an extraordinary meal.

There were plenty of canned goods, frozen meats and vegetables, as well as onions and potatoes. If only a cookbook would appear. Admittedly, she wanted to impress him. She'd make a casserole. Mixing a bunch of food together and heating it up in the oven couldn't be too difficult.

Assuming that Clay, like most men, wanted his dinner to include meat, she took a package from the freezer and defrosted it in the microwave. That proved to be a drippy mess, but at least she had meat to add to the casserole, albeit mystery meat. The package was not labeled.

The sun dipped below the surrounding mountaintops late that afternoon. By the time Clay entered the cabin, the sky was dark. He moved slower than a snail. Happy but exhausted. He collapsed into a chair at the table and sniffed the air. "That smells different. Good, but unusual."

"It's a casserole."

"Ah, one of your mom's famous Yuma recipes?"

"I doubt it." Should she come clean and confess her lack of culinary experience? "Why don't you wash up and remove a few layers of the mud and dust that's clinging to you?

"Now you're sounding like *my* mother."

How should she react? Was that a compliment or a dig?

He noticed the perplexing look on her face and bent down to kiss her gently on the lips. "And I love my mother. I just don't like the farm and the chickens."

She kissed him back and then pushed him into the small bathroom. "Dinner will be on the table in ten minutes."

The table was bleak. Winn vowed to make tomorrow night's dining experience more palatable and visually pleasing. She'd drive the Jeep into Telluride and pick up a candle or two and a pretty vase. She would attempt to buy a bottle of wine.

Neither ate very much. Not because the meal tasted awful, but it had an odd, peculiar flavor. Lucky loved it, so it didn't go to waste.

"Let's hit the hay."

"Can I assume that's cowboy talk for going to bed?"

"Yep." Clay was totally into his cowboy persona.

"I'll clean up while you take our little buddy out for his evening walk."

Clay finished the walk before she completed her dish duties. He stood behind her and pressed his warm, firm body against hers. "The dishes can wait until morning. I can't," he whispered into her ear. Then he took her hand and led her to the bed that was only five feet from where they stood.

"Just give me a minute." She went into the bathroom and closed the door. This could be the night that would change her life forever. The least she could do was brush her teeth.

She turned out the light, patted Lucky on the head, and slipped into bed with Clay. He lay on his side, breathing softly. When she stroked his back, he sighed.

"Clay?" He was sound asleep. Now it was her turn to sigh. She snuggled up behind him to keep warm. Tonight would not be *that* night. She, too, was tired and only seconds from dozing off when he mumbled something. What had he said in the innocence of sleep? It sounded a lot like, "I love you."

Chapter Nine

December 22

Clay left the car keys with Winn, and she left the dog with him. Not sure how the canine would react to the horses or the horses to him, he kept Lucky on a leash and tied it to the post closest to where he was working. Margie was okay with that, and the dog behaved well. He didn't bark at anything or anyone. He sat still, his eyes following every action with interest.

"Today, we're working with Braveheart. He's a former racehorse who lost more than he won. His moronic and cruel owners thought beating him would make him faster. Their treatment of the horse turned him into a kicker and a biter. About a month ago, he came to us malnourished and afraid of people."

Hearing the horse's story made Clay angry. How

could anyone hurt an animal, especially a horse as majestic as this one? He wouldn't mind showing the owners a thing or two. Give them a taste of their own medicine. Oh, yeah. He'd like that.

Braveheart reared up.

"Clay, whatever you're thinking, get it out of your head. You're spooking the horse. Our job here at the rescue is to help these horses through their fears. We need to be non-threatening with soothing voices, friendly eyes, and calm thoughts. Got it?"

"Yes, ma'am." Until now, Clay had no idea a horse could sense his thoughts, and he immediately switched his internal gears to feelings of a positive nature. He'd do his best to hide his angry thoughts toward animal abusers until he was a good distance from any of the horses.

The morning flew by. They were successful getting Braveheart within inches of their open, treat-filled palms. That was progress, though the slowness of it tried Clay's patience.

Back from her shopping trip, Winn called out, "Margie," as she ran toward them. "The woman in your office asked me to get you. She said there was an emergency. A horse needs to be picked up right away."

Without replying, Margie sprinted to the house. Clay, Winn, and Lucky followed at a slower pace. By the time they caught up, Ms. Horsewoman and one of her ranch hands were hooking up the trailer to her truck. "Take the rest of the day off. I'll see you tomor-row." Then she was gone.

Clay frowned, disappointed that she hadn't asked him to come along. On the other hand, Winn was elated and suggested they pack a meal, bundle up, and go for a hike today.

Happy with her productive morning, Winn bubbled over with joy. Her brief trip to town had been a success. Their next dinner in the cabin would be tasty, as well as attractive. Anticipating an adventure exploring the mountain that rose up behind the ranch, she'd purchased the makings for a perfect outdoor, take-along meal. When they stopped to rest and enjoy a snack, she'd surprise Clay with the goodies she'd brought.

The pièce de résistance? While walking Lucky after her trip to town, she found a trailhead beyond the northern fence line of the ranch. Could this day get any better? Clay would be blown away by her accom-plishments.

Hiking wasn't high on Clay's list of things to do today, but he knew this might be the only free time during his ranch fantasy week that he and Winn could have an outdoor adventure together.

"I hope the horse is all right," Winn said. "The woman in the office seemed upset and said time was of the essence. I wonder if that means the animal is injured."

"We'll have to wait until they return to find out." Clay, still disappointed he'd not been included in this rescue, needed to show a little enthusiasm for the upcoming hike with Winn. She deserved his attention.

Standing in front of the trailhead sign, Clay asked, "Which trail sounds good to you?" She selected the three-mile hike. "This trail goes uphill. Let me carry your pack. It looks heavy."

It was heavy. The plastic water bottles added a few pounds, but the pack would get lighter as the day progressed. The mid-day temperature felt warm, comfortable. Possibly because they were bundled up in winter jackets, hats, and gloves, and they were hiking uphill. Clay said he thought the cloud cover added to their comfort, holding in what little heat radiated from the earth this time of year and at this altitude.

They'd hiked about a mile and a half when they came to a fork in the trail and another trail marker. They stopped to catch their breath, rehydrate, and decide which way to go. The backpack rattled with every step Clay took. "What have you got in here?"

"Essentials. Oh, look! There's a squirrel." Winn

gleefully pointed at the small black animal with a furry tail. This was the first wild animal sighting of the day.

At the mere sound of the word, Lucky's tail made excited circles in the air. The second he saw it, he took off. Clay ran after the dog, and Winn watched and giggled. The squirrel reached an area comprised of medium and large boulders. It jumped from boulder to boulder easily. Lucky scrambled with some difficulty—his paws kept slipping down between the big rocks—but not without unrestrained enthusiasm. Clay struggled to keep up. The action, the comical parade, happened so quickly, that the trio's sudden disappearance took her by surprise.

"Clay? Lucky? Come back!" She heard nothing except birds whistling. Cautiously, she walked toward the boulders. She hadn't gone far when Lucky bounded back happy and proud. Clay moved slower, happy but limping. "What's the matter? Are you hurt?"

"I'll be fine, and the SQ survived."

"The SQ?"

"Yes. We will never call *that* animal by its name as long as our dog is within hearing distance. The code word for the animal is SQ, at least until Lucky is on to our deception. So, where were we?"

"We were choosing a prong of the fork. I say we stick with our original choice, the three-mile trail. We must be almost to the end of that one, don't you think?"

"I hope you're right. I'm getting hungry and wouldn't mind sitting for a while."

"We could go back. You shouldn't be walking on an injured leg."

"I'm fine," he insisted. When Winn saw the grimace on his face as he took another step, her caregiving nature kicked in. She pulled the pack from Clay's back, slung it over her own shoulder, and then hooked arms with him to lend support. "Hey, I'm a strong, healthy man who can take care of himself. I'm not one of your nursing home patients." His words were worse than a punch in the gut. Her kindness had backfired.

Clay and Winn moved on, though slower. Neither spoke. Instead of dashing ahead of them, Lucky stuck to the path and followed. The trail became steeper, rockier, and less obvious. Either they'd taken a wrong turn, or this was the path less traveled. They weren't chilled despite the cold. The exertion expended on the uphill climb produced sweat on Clay and glistening perspiration on Winn.

When a picturesque, level patch of forest appeared off to the left of the trail, they made a unanimous decision to stop. This would be as far as they'd go. They took off their warm jackets and sat on them in lieu of a blanket. Winn emptied her pack laying out her ingredients, the folding tin oven, a small saucepan, matches, and a can of Sterno. Feeling proud and needed, she began to prepare a small, trailside meal.

Before the ramen noodles softened completely, more clouds rolled in, and with them came a few snowflakes. Winn, so entranced by the sight of snow, paid no attention to her trembling, shivering body. Clay picked up her jacket from the ground and helped her into it. Then, he put his own coat back on. The temperature dropped, and the flakes multiplied. They huddled close to the tiny Sterno flame as it warmed the noodles. Winn poured most of the water from the pan and added the piñon nuts and Italian seasoning, along with Romano cheese.

Clay blew out the flame when the food was ready to eat. They each had their own fork and ate the ramen creation directly from the small saucepan. The meal wouldn't win any awards but supplied the needed nourishment. They mixed the last spoonful of the concoction with Lucky's dried food, which disappeared so fast that they wondered if he even tasted his dinner.

Winn wiped their only cooking utensil with a paper towel and lit the flame again. She wasn't finished. Pleased with herself, she poured water into the pan, squeezed and picked out the seeds from a handful of fresh cranberries, and dropped them in.

"Hey, babe. I think we should get back."

Lucky told them he agreed by yipping and making a new woofing sound. "He's expanding his vocabulary." Her comment produced a brief chuckle from Clay, breaking his near silence. Determined to let nothing rain or snow her parade today, she continued. "Just a few more minutes, all right? You're going to love this tea. It will keep us warm, especially after I add a few drops of apricot brandy. And, in case you hadn't noticed, I am a very happy camper."

Before they finished sipping the cranberry tea, snowflakes the size of quarters fell from the darkening sky. They packed up quickly and headed down the steep, rocky part of the trail. They let Lucky lead the way, believing his internal homing devices were superior to theirs. They hoped he'd get them back to the ranch despite the fading light and nearly invisible path.

Their hopes vanished when Lucky led them back to the spot where they'd rested and ate. Clay bent down to rub the dog's ears. "That's okay, Lucky. We couldn't have done any better ourselves."

Winn moved close to Clay. He encircled her with his arms, and the warmth generated by their closeness felt heavenly. "As good as this feels, we've got to get moving and walk out of here. Unless we stumble on a cabin or a cave, we won't last the night." He saw the horrified look on her face. Clay realized she had no idea that her beautiful, wished-for snow could be deadly.

Attempting to sound encouraging, he added, "At least it's all downhill from here. We might get down the mountain faster than we hiked up."

"That's true, but it is downhill in almost every direction, and only one way leads to the ranch."

With no other option, they agreed to keep moving

and take their chances. While walking, they stayed warm except for Winn's feet. She'd worn her sturdiest shoes, but they weren't for serious hiking or snow. He knew she must be hurting. His leg wasn't feeling good either. Some fantasy this turned out to be—lost and stranded in a snowstorm.

He'd have loved the storm if he and Winn watched it while sitting in front of a roaring fire in a cozy cabin. That vision produced a short-lived flash of warmth in his body. He turned to look at her, making sure she was close behind. She was amazing. She hadn't complained. Not once.

The air was still. Thank goodness the wind was not blowing. Only the sounds of their shoes crunching on the snow and their own breaths puffing in and out from the exertion of their trek could be heard. Between the heavy snow and lack of daylight, visibility was near zero. Clay was shocked when Winn called out from behind him, "I think I see a trail marker!"

She pushed ahead of him and hurried toward it. Clay thought it was probably a small tree trunk. But when he caught up with her, he saw he was wrong. He'd never been so happy to be wrong in his entire life. This sign meant they were only one and a half miles from the ranch and the warmth and safety it would provide. They were moving in the right direction.

The pole that held the sign with the arrows and trail names stood straight up from the ground, but the sign with the needed information lay on the ground, partially covered by the snow.

"That's odd. It didn't seem loose the last time we stood here looking at it."

Clay thought for a moment. "Maybe it's not the same trail marker."

Winn knelt down and brushed the snow from the sign. "I think it is the same one, but we have a new problem." She handed it to Clay. The sign hadn't fallen off. Someone cut it from the pole with a saw. Who would do that?

Chapter Ten

Still December 22

Not knowing which direction to go, Clay admitted to himself that they were lost. They couldn't retrace their steps if they wanted to. The indentations their shoes had made in the snow were already covered up. Clay rubbed his throbbing leg and felt the swelling.

"Winn, do we have any matches left?"

She nodded. "Matches, about half a can of the Sterno, and some brandy." A sweet smile spread across her face.

There's far more to this woman than I'd realized.

"Good, because we will take a break, rest, and light that little can of fire for a while." He started to sit down when Winn pulled him back up.

Looking at Lucky, she yelled, "Squirrel!" The

excited dog bounded through the deep snow, then stopped and sniffed frantically. He'd led them to the boulders where the black squirrel had sent Lucky and Clay on a wild goose chase a few hours earlier. The squirrel's scent lingered.

"I'd forgotten that an out-cropping and the SQ event were so near the trail marker. Just the other side of those boulders is a spot with some thick bushes and an overhang where we can rest and keep warm for a while." Thanks to Winn's quick thinking, there was hope.

They agreed to hunker down for only fifteen minutes, hold each other tightly, and sip the rest of the brandy. After that, they'd continue their downhill hike and pray they'd find the ranch. Lucky snuggled in between them. He was the best blanket the two snow-bound hikers could have hoped for.

Winn broke the silence, the stillness. "Clay, why were you late that first night of my fantasy vacation?"

He hesitated, not wanting to tell her the truth. "I don't like to fly."

"You didn't answer my question. There must be more to it."

"You got me there. Let's make a deal. I have questions for you too. I'll answer yours, if you answer mine."

Now Winn was the one hesitating. "Not sure that's fair. You know my question, but I don't know yours."

"Okay, here's my first one. What's your real name? That should be easy enough."

"You're right. It is easy. My name is Winter, but no one calls me that."

"Winter. Hmm. I'll call you by your real name. It's unusual and beautiful, like you. Here's another question. Since you are able to quote amazing things from books and your vocabulary is so far beyond mine, you must have read millions of books with big words."

"That's a statement, not a question."

He followed up with his question. "Why didn't you bring any books with you? Or at least an e-book reader, something?"

"I brought a dictionary. That's a book."

"No. Not really." Suddenly, her face held the saddest expression he'd ever seen. What had he said that brought on that feeling?

Her voice lowered, and she looked away. "I didn't bring any books because I'm not a good reader. I never was. School was very hard for me because I have dyslexia."

Clay couldn't believe that was true. She appeared to be so well-read. "I thought people with dyslexia just wrote letters backward."

"Many people think that, but there's a lot more to it. Let's just say that though I'm not well-read, I am well-listened. I've listened to hundreds of books on tape."

He whispered into her ear, "None of that matters to me. You're the most wonderful woman I've ever known. You're kind, beautiful, and caring."

She stopped him. "And you don't like to fly because . . .?"

Without any hesitation, he confessed. "My terrible fear of heights includes flying. I traveled to Denver on a train rather than use the plane ticket given to me by the escort service. It took longer, so I was late."

"And that's why you wouldn't look down from the rotating restaurant at the top of the hotel, huh?"

He nodded. "Yes, that among other things." The proverbial light went on in his head. A moment of sudden insight arrived. "And you mixed up the time of your flight and read 5:20 instead of 2:50. Am I right?"

They'd learned more about each other sitting together for fifteen minutes in the middle of a snow-storm than during the previous week. Relieved by their confessions, they needed to get on the move before the sky turned completely black. There'd be no moon or stars to guide them tonight.

Upon moving out from under the crude rock shelter, Lucky stood motionless and growled. Winn looked in all directions for what might be causing the dog to act that way, but she saw only snow falling sideways. Along with the darkness, the wind chilled them to the bone. There was no denying they were in a dangerous situation.

"Do we dare try to find our way through this white-out?" She knew the answer before she asked her question.

Clay took a deep breath. "We don't stand a chance of making it to the ranch or any other safe place."

"We can't give up. There's fuel left in the Sterno can. We have matches. Let's fortify our rock shelter with tree boughs and branches. We should be okay if we can keep a fire going until morning. Right?"

"I like the way you think," Clay said, holding her face in his gloved hands. "I love you, Miss Wahlberg. I really do. And we will survive." He kissed her gently on the lips before walking away in search of wood, but when Winn saw how badly he limped, she ran after him.

"I think it would be best if you stayed and constructed a stronger shelter for us from nearby branches." She shouted to make her words heard above the howling gale. "I'll gather fuel for our fire."

He shook his head. "I don't like that idea, not at all."

"I'll shout your name every few minutes, so you'll know I'm all right. You shout my name back. I won't go far. Build our shelter and make a space for our fire."

"Okay, but take Lucky with you."

Winn and the dog headed in the direction of the trail marker. The sign on the ground would be her first piece of firewood. The pole would be her point of reference, as well as where'd she'd pile anything burnable. She'd do her best to keep it in sight.

"Clay!"

"Winter!"

Their safety plan was working, but it confused Lucky. He kept running back and forth when the familiar names were called out. At least the running kept him warm.

Winn's pile by the pole was almost sufficient. One more armful of wood should do it. Taking in a few chilly, deep breaths, she managed to find the strength to make one last dash into the trees, knowing that this grueling task was nearly complete.

"Clay!"

"Winter!"

Soon, she'd be snuggling by a fire in a makeshift cave with a wonderful man. She began to hum, thinking the words, the sun will come out to—From out of nowhere, a gloved hand came from behind and covered her mouth, muffling her spontaneous scream. Her struggle to free herself proved futile.

Confusion. Pain. Panic. What the Hell!

She was powerless as her attacker pushed her further into the dense trees, keeping her mouth covered tightly. Breathing was difficult, screaming for help, impossible. Unable to get a good look at her assailant made the situation more terrifying. Her thoughts went wild. Who would be crazy enough to wander around in this weather? What could anyone want from her, especially out here on a mountain, in the woods, in a life-threatening storm?

He shoved her body against a tree, face-first into the

trunk. "Hands behind your back. Now!" She tried to turn, to run, to scream. "I wouldn't do that if I were you, or I'll come back and finish off your imposter of a boyfriend." He sounded proud of himself, as if he were doing a good deed. "Hell, I may do that anyway." After tying her hands, he tied another rope securely around her waist and placed his hand over her mouth again. They were on the move like an awkward, four-legged creature.

What could she do? Think. Think.

Winn's attempts to pull free failed, her strength all but gone. Desperate, she bit his hand and, though it likely did little damage through the glove, the hand jerked away from her mouth. She choked out the words, "What do you want?"

"You," was all the male voice said. He continued pushing her, using a firm grip on her neck. Her mouth remained uncovered, making it easier to breathe.

"Can we rest for a while? I can't take another step." She was exhausted and felt her chances of escaping were better if they stopped to rest. Feeling like a lamb being led to slaughter, she asked, "What's your hurry?"

"Got a deadline. A car's waiting. Keep walking."

"How do you know which way to go? The snow is covering everything." If she could keep him talking, he might not hurt her. That was a strategy she'd seen kidnapped victims use. At least in movies and novels.

His sinister laugh came first, then, "I learned a thing

or two from Hansel and Gretel. Now, shut the fuck up, my red-headed money maker."

She needed a new plan. Keeping this man talking might not work. The words he spoke were disturbing, scary, and made her heart race. *I wish he would shut the fuck up.* He remained behind her, pushing her down the mountain. With the approaching darkness and heavy snowfall, visibility was severely limited. The man had said he was in a hurry, which could work to her advantage. She had a plan. Counting silently to three, she purposely fell to the ground in front of him. He tripped over her and rolled several feet. Winn's plan might have worked if he hadn't managed to grab her leg. She couldn't get away, but she saw his face.

"It's you!"

Chapter Eleven

Still December 22

The crude lean-to Clay constructed against the boulder was ready for occupancy. He shivered. He didn't want to light the fire until Winn returned with the additional, life-sustaining wood. Where was she? Their all's-good call worked for a while but his last two calls received no reply. He tried again. "Winter!" Silence.

Not hearing her call back, Lucky remained with Clay and began making a call of his own. The dog howled right in Clay's face. "I'm worried, too, but what can we do?" The animal turned in circles and pawed the leader of his pack relentlessly. He knew something. "You want to find her, huh? Well, so do I. Let's go."

Leaving nothing behind, he slung the full pack over his shoulder and followed the excited dog away from their shelter. Adrenaline surged through his body. He ignored the pain in his leg and thought only of finding Winter.

Lucky slowed down as they approached the trail marker post. Clay was amazed at the large pile of dead wood she'd collected. He called out again. "Winter!" Nothing. Lucky barked, urging him to follow. Keeping up with the dog was challenging. Fortunately, he'd stop, turn around, and wait a few seconds for Clay to catch up before taking off again.

Clay had no choice but to trust the dog's superior scent-finding nose. What if they couldn't find her? What if they found her and she was hurt? How would they survive a cold, snowy night on the mountain without the small warmth of their shelter and a fire? Could he find his way back to that crude shelter? It was too late to try to find the ranch. Focus. Focus. Just find Winter.

Lucky came to a sudden stop and crouched low in the snow. Clay needed the rest, though stopping brought a shivering chill back to his body. When he heard the dog's faint growl, his heart raced, the adrenaline flowed again. He listened and steadied himself for what lay ahead, knowing it wouldn't be good. Footfalls crunched in the snow, distressed sighs hung in the air. It had to be Winter, but she wasn't alone.

Lucky headed toward the sounds, the smells, in total silence. Clay attempted to do the same. They were close when they heard two people talking. Yes! One of them was Winn. He rubbed Lucky's head in a premature celebration. He wanted to run to her, save her, but Lucky wanted to keep listening. Okay, he could do that, but only for a minute.

"Why do you want me? Where are you taking me?"

"I'll answer a couple of questions, then we've got to go. I'm behind schedule."

He explained that the moment he saw her in the lounge at the hotel, he knew she was exactly the woman he needed to fulfill an order. If he delivered the goods, he'd receive $25,000, money he would risk everything to obtain.

"I can't deliver damaged goods, so I won't hurt you.

"You're a sex trafficker? You're selling me to someone?"

"It's not as bad as it sounds. A filthy-rich sheik wants a woman that looks just like you. You'll live in luxury."

"No! I'd be living in captivity." Her hands still tied, she screamed and lunged at him. She'd not give up without a fight.

Lucky lunged, too, and Clay was only seconds behind. Three against one—they could do this. Lucky grabbed one of the offender's arms firmly in his strong jaws. Clay pummeled the guy with his fists and got a few good kicks in too. Winn twisted around and managed to unwind the rope that had kept her from getting too far from this deranged, evil man. Clay used that rope to bind the guy's hands and feet and tie him to a tree. He wouldn't be going anywhere for a while.

With her assailant unable to move, Clay quickly freed Winn's hands. "Oh, Winter, my beautiful, brave woman. I couldn't imagine what I'd do if we hadn't found you." They stood wrapped in each other's arms as if they were one, sharing warm kisses and comforting hugs.

"You saved me. Thank you. That guy was going to—"

He put a finger to her lips. "Shh. I know. We heard. Don't think about that, but thank Lucky. He deserves all the credit for finding you. We sure chose the right name for our dog." They knelt down by Lucky and engaged in a group hug. "I hope he can guide us back to the wood pile you made and our tiny shelter. We will—"

Before he'd finished his sentence, the dog took off running in the wrong direction. "Lucky, come back," Clay called, his tone plagued with distress. Their brief celebration of love and life vanished like the ghost of Christmas past.

Looking on the bright side, Winn suggested that Lucky's departure might have been a blessing in disguise. It forced them to stay put. They distanced themselves just enough to keep an eye on the ruthless kidnapper but not feel the evil surrounding him.

They'd have to make do without a shelter. Some of the items they needed to build a fire were in Winn's pack. And they had snow, lots of snow. They built a three-foot-high wall of snow in the shape of a horseshoe and then gathered dead branches for the fire and evergreen boughs to make a bed. Clay started the fire at the opening of the horseshoe. Once it got going, they snuggled together for warmth and emotional comfort, helping each other stay awake and alert.

"I hope Lucky is all right. I really love that dog." Clay nodded his agreement and gave her a deep, steamy kiss. Though they continued to shiver, they were warmer than they'd been in several hours. The fire's glow brightened, and its heat-giving nature increased with each piece of wood Clay added.

Then, the unthinkable happened. Their tiny glimmer of hope vanished. The life-saving fire turned against them, becoming their new enemy. Its heat warmed their wall of snow to its melting point. The snow that had clung to the branches of a Blue Spruce growing just behind them became wet and heavy and crashed down, covering them and the fire. They brushed the chilling wet snow from each other's heads and shoulders and then scooped away at the pile where the fire had been. Not a single live spark remained.

Without the protective wall and the warm fire, they were doomed. That chilled-to-the-bone feeling returned within seconds. Teeth chattering, Clay stated, "Oh, babe, we need a miracle."

Shaking so hard, Winn's body ached as if she'd been pummeled with icicles. "It is the season for miracles."

Her words puffed out in a whisper. They clung to each other, out of ideas, unable to move until a maniacal laugh echoed through the darkness. They'd almost forgotten about their prisoner.

"Winter, did he have any supplies with him? Matches, a phone, anything that might keep us alive?"

"I'm not sure. I didn't get a chance to look at him or any objects he might be carrying until I tripped him. By then it was dark." She continued thinking. "Oh, wait. He said something about Hansel and Gretel and finding his way down the mountain. I don't know what he meant by that. Maybe nothing."

"Or maybe something."

She snuggled close, needing more of his warmth. "In keeping with our current fairytale theme, you spill the beans, and I'll listen for the magic." They kissed and pretended there was hope.

"Okay. Here come the beans. I think he must have some kind of GPS device that allows him to retrace the steps he took on his ascent. If we could get that from him, we might . . ."

Unable to wait until he finished his thought, Winn interrupted, "Clay, listen. I think I hear the magic. Barking, yes, I hear barking. That's our magic."

"I do hear something, but it could be a coyote."

"That's Lucky. I'd know his bark anywhere."

They both shouted, "Lucky? Over here. We're over here." Lucky bounded into view and jumped into their arms. He wasn't alone. There was more to this magical miracle. Behind him were four horses. Two had riders, two followed along. The riders wore trail hats containing LED lights to show the way. The lights blinded Clay and Winn for a moment.

"Margie? Is that you?" Clay asked, hoping this was a friendly rescue party.

"None other."

She gave them each a thick wool blanket and sips of hot coffee from a thermos.

"Let's get you two off this mountain and into the main house before we all freeze to death. Then, we'll talk about how in the world you got lost in a snowstorm."

"Sounds good, but there's three of us. You knew that, right?"

"No." Margie sounded surprised. "We're here because you were missing, and then your dog and this guy came to my door, each raising a ruckus. Long story short, we saddled up and followed your dog. They're often smarter than people, you know?"

"Yes, we know," Winn replied.

"Good. Get your friend over here, and let's mount up. You two okay with riding double?"

"We're good with riding double, but the friend is not a friend. He's a monster who tried to kidnap Winter."

Winn added what she knew. "He's a dangerous criminal involved in human trafficking. Right now, he's tied up securely and slightly damaged."

The man on the other horse spoke for the first time.

Looking right at Winn, he asked, "Is he armed?"

"I don't know. I never saw anything but ropes."

"Margie, call the sheriff on your satellite phone and ask him to meet us at the ranch."

"Will do."

The man dismounted and turned to Clay. "You want to show me where you've put this dude?"

"Sure. Do I know you? You look familiar."

He offered his hand to Clay. "My name is Martin, and I work for The Fantasy Maker."

Clay's jaw dropped, and Winn felt as shocked as he looked. "Weren't you the limo driver?"

He nodded but said no more.

"Come on. Let's get this guy on a horse before the temperature gets any colder." Margie ordered.

Lucky followed the horses and their riders down the mountain. His energy depleted from a job well done, he ambled toward the ranch. Snow no longer fell, and a slice of the moon, plus a few bright stars, shone at the edge of the remaining clouds. Now and then, the man tied to the horse grumbled a cuss word. A few pleasant sounds echoed through the crisp, fresh air. Horse hooves on the snow, the creaking of leather, and Martin softly singing Christmas carols.

Riding down the mountain on the back of a horse felt surreal. Many questions needed answers, but that was for another time. Tonight, Winn wanted to experience all the peace, joy, and love that Clay and the Christmas season had to offer.

Chapter Twelve

December 23

The sun's rays beamed down from the top of the mountain and through the window, waking Winn. She rubbed her eyes and yawned. The smell of the coffee Clay poured made her smile. He'd lit a fire in the small woodstove, the only source of heat in the cabin.

"Good morning, sweetheart. We have the day off and a dinner invitation."

"All right," she groaned, sounding like a frog in pain. "I had the worst dream. We were stranded in a blizzard, and a guy tried to kidnap me and . . ."

"That was no dream, Winter. That was last night."

Clay brought over a mug of coffee. Winn bolted upright, suddenly wide-awake. "You're right. That was real, and we survived." Glancing around the small cabin's interior, something was missing. Lucky. She was afraid to ask. He'd had a rough time too. "Where's Lucky?"

"He's out having a ball. After his performance yesterday, Margie gave him free run of the ranch. She said not only was he a natural, but also the horses enjoyed his company." Clay climbed back into bed and positioned her head on his shoulder.

They spoke of yesterday's joys and uncertainties, avoiding words like peril, danger, and near-death, sharing details about their time apart on the mountain. Winn couldn't take much more and said, "Let's not talk about it. I want to forget the whole thing happened. So, what will we do on your day off?"

"At noon, we have a date with a doctor. According to Martin, the Fantasy Maker insisted. After that appointment, we will be interviewed by several local and federal law enforcement people. Tonight, we're expected at the main house at seven for dinner with Margie, two of her top teammates, and Martin."

"Hmm. That doesn't sound like a day off, but we have a couple of hours with nothing to do." She struggled to come up with a word to encompass all she felt at the moment—love and lust, with a side of mischief. Was there such a word? She'd check her dictionary later. In the meantime, she focused on love. She loved Clay and was ready to let him know he meant everything to her even if the feeling wasn't mutual.

She took the coffee cup from his hand and placed it on the rustic bedside table. Face-to-face under the covers, she initiated the kissing, feeling confident her lips would not disappoint. Her boldness escalated based upon noticing the hard bulge that pressed against her from under Clay's Scotch Plaid flannel boxers. Knowing he wanted her, she explored his bare chest with her hands, and the kissing continued. She'd envisioned an experience like this for years, but the right man had not come along until now.

She winced at the throbbing pain coming from her wrists but told Clay she was fine. He initiated a gentle roll of their bodies that placed Winn on her back, looking into his face. He gazed down at her, his eyes shining with love. The rest of him conveyed lust. She was ready and willing for the ultimate closeness. They'd been through more in two weeks than most couples ever experience.

She closed her eyes when he kissed her neck, her ears, even the tip of her nose. Her aches and pains took a backseat to his sensual touches. If only this morning and this feeling could last forever. Imagine bliss every day. Was that even possible? Realistic? In her travels around the town of Yuma, she never saw another couple with that look of love in their eyes.

"Winter? You're thinking too much right now."

Perplexed, she inquired, "How do you know that?"

"Your face. You're wearing your thinking look, and I intend to remove it."

She giggled. He was right. This was not the time to overwork her brain. How did he intend to remove that look? She didn't wonder for long. He reached under the covers in search of the bottom hem of her long, silky nightgown. In doing so, his hands slid up the length of her legs from her calves, past her knees, to the inside of her thighs, where they lingered.

He pushed the covers to the bottom of the bed, then straddled her hips while slowly lifting the nightgown higher, exposing her breasts, and finally, over her head. With it went her habit of thinking. Winn loved how he kept his eyes on her as he stood, removed his boxers, and tossed them across the room. With the distractions of thinking and sleepwear gone, they focused on each other.

Clay was the more playful and adventurous one in bed. She liked that about him, but two could play. She'd wait for inspiration, the just-right moment. Mixed with passionate kisses and sensual touching was some tickling and laughter. During one of those fun, silly moments, she said, "We've only known each other for two weeks. Maybe we should wait a little longer before we go further." She meant to tease, to kid around. Or did she?

"You're so sensible and right. We should wait—until tomorrow." Laughing, the heat of the moment decreased by a few degrees. They enjoyed holding each other, skin-to-skin, heart-to-heart.

A doctor from Telluride drove to the ranch to conduct physicals on Winn and Clay. He wrapped Clay's bruised knee in an ace bandage and advised him to stop chasing squirrels, dogs, or anything else he might get a sudden urge to run after.

He bandaged Winn's wrists where the ropes had rubbed them raw and then soaked her feet in warm water. He instructed her to do the same several times a day for the next three days. Her toes had a touch of frostnip, explaining why her feet were so white and numb. The doctor assured her they would heal.

He gave them each a semi-clean bill of health. Before walking out the door, the doctor handed each of his patients a card with an invitation to call his cell number if any medical issues worsened or surfaced. He added, "Keep warm and get some rest."

Clay kept the woodstove burning while Winn soaked. He knew she'd rather be taking care of him than sitting still with her feet soaking in water. To keep her occupied, he picked up a book of short stories from the tiny shelf and began to read to her. His distraction worked like a charm until someone knocked on the cabin's door.

Barely sticking her head in, Margie delivered her message. "Clay, Winn. The sheriff, a detective, and an FBI agent are waiting for you in the main house."

"Okay, thanks. We'll be right over." Clay's voice showed a lack of interest, wishing these interviews would disappear. "Already, we are not able to follow the doctor's orders. Let's dry your feet before we head out into the cold."

Margie showed them into the dining room, where two men, one woman, and Martin waited. Winn smiled politely, and Clay shook everyone's hand. "Hi, Martin. This is a surprise."

"I'll be heading out Christmas Day. Considering all that's happened, I thought I'd stick around and make sure there are no more glitches regarding your time here."

Margie poured six cups of tea and set a plate of oatmeal cookies on the table before leaving the room. It seemed there was no time for pleasantries; the sheriff pressed RECORD on his device, and the interview began.

Winn had more to say than Clay because she'd spent the most time with the suspect. In addition to answering questions, she asked a few of her own. "What is his name? He never told me."

Agent Meyers nodded at the two law enforcement men at the table before answering Winn's question. "We're still trying to find out. He's not talking."

Winn spoke of her ordeal, from the moment they'd met in the bar to when he'd been put on a horse and taken down the mountain. "The man must have been stalking me ever since that first night, waiting for an opportunity to take me without drawing the attention or notice of others." After making that comment, she wondered if he might have spotted her at the airport.

"All those times when our dog Lucky acted strangely and growled for no reason, we are certain he knew this man was close by and up to no good." After Clay added his two cents, they were asked to recall when and where they were every time Lucky tried to warn them. A few ideas came to mind, though some were approximations and others were mere guesses.

When neither Winn nor Clay could think of any additional details, they were excused from the meeting. "Come on, Winter." He paused, then winked. "Let's follow the doctor's orders and get some rest before dinner."

Clay's fantasy vacation was officially over tomorrow night. The following day they would head home, each going their separate ways. A profound sadness invaded Winn's heart and soul. She'd had the most thrilling two weeks of her life here in Colorado and wished her time with Clay could go on forever.

Snap out of it! Get over it! Be thankful for the good times you had. That's what she told herself over and over. But picking up where'd she'd left off in Yuma, living with her mother and father and without Clay, would be difficult.

Wanting to look especially pretty for tonight's dinner, she dressed in the gray wool slacks, the cream-colored blouse, and the hunter green sweater she'd purchased in Denver. While applying mascara and lip color, Clay whistled like a construction worker in a hard hat and put his arms around her waist. "Tonight will be our first social event as a couple."

She nodded, unable to summon a smile because this night might also be their last. "Is it time to go? I'm as ready as I'll ever be." They fed Lucky his evening meal and headed to the main house, Margie's home.

Clay clanked the horseshoe-shaped doorknocker and heard Margie holler, "Come on in. The door's open." The living area was warm, toasty, and inviting. A fire crackled in the fireplace, and a delicious aroma drifted in from the kitchen. Margie entered carrying a tray. "Dinner will be ready in about thirty minutes. In the meantime, help yourself to these jalapeño poppers and sparkling water. I guarantee you'll want some water." She laughed and headed back to the kitchen.

Martin chuckled. "I made the poppers."

Clay and Winn glanced at each other and shrugged. Somehow, Martin didn't seem like the cooking type, especially in someone else's kitchen. After biting into one, Winn gulped down some water and asked, "Is this an old family recipe?"

"No," was Martin's answer.

Clay joined the food conversation. "Wow! These are hot. Hot, but good. Is this your own recipe?"

Martin shook his head. Grinning, he admitted, "I learned how to make them on a cruise ship."

Another knock at the door put an end to their discussion of the hot poppers. Randy, the barn manager, and Shellie, the office manager, had arrived, each carrying a bottle of wine.

Margie introduced everyone and insisted the poppers needed to be eaten before sitting down at the large dining table. They all nibbled on the hot snack, downed plenty of cold, sparkling water, and talked about horses. Clay and Winn learned that two new horses, both Spanish Barbs, would arrive in a week. One was in dire need of nourishment and the company of kind, soothing humans. The second one needed a forever home and had therapy horse potential.

Margie had decorated a living pine tree with silver balls, red ribbons, and animal ornaments made from pinecones. Christmas music played softly throughout the house, and twinkling white lights framed each window.

Winn, mesmerized by the beauty around her, whispered into Clay's ear, "My Christmases in Yuma never felt like this. We had a tree and presents every year, but the weather was hot and dry. No crackling fires or snow. I feel as if I'm living a fairytale life, and I love it." Pausing, she looked into Clay's eyes. "I didn't know what I was missing until now."

"Dinner is served!"

Margie sat at the head of the table, pointing at

Martin to sit at the other end. Clay and Winn sat next to each other, with Randy and Shellie facing them. They joined hands before serving plates were passed, waiting for the blessing to be said. Winn was certain she'd seen Martin and Margie wink at each other. That was odd.

The blessing was quite short. Margie paused, giving the impression grace was over. Clay squeezed Winn's hand, and with bowed heads, they peeked around the table. Margie and Martin were smiling at each other. *What's with those two?*

To their surprise, the blessing continued. "And we hope that Clay and Winn will accept my offer to stay an extra week with us here on the ranch. Amen. Dig in." Food was passed, wine was poured, and everyone ate as if nothing unusual had just occurred. Everyone except Clay and Winn. They were overcome with shock and joy.

"We need to talk," Winn said softly, wondering how she could accept Margie's astonishing offer.

"We sure do." His eyebrows wiggled up and down, and his smile conveyed delight and a touch of mischief.

A simple meal of meatloaf, mashed potatoes, and broccoli was followed by coffee and homemade apple pie with ice cream. Before leaving, they thanked Margie for the wonderful dinner and the unexpected offer and bid goodnight to Randy, Shellie, and Martin.

Lucky greeted them, his tail forming wild circles in the air. Winn made cups of hot tea. Sitting next to Clay, she began the necessary conversation. "Clay, I thought we'd be leaving here and heading home on Christmas Day. Your fantasy vacation was to be over at midnight, and the imaginary second week of my conference would be over too. I'm not sure what to do."

"You could tell your parents the truth."

"They'll be upset if I'm not home for Christmas and angry when they find out how many lies I've told. I can't face that right now, nor can I handle another week without a paycheck."

"Okay. Get comfortable while I get a fire going. I've got an idea."

Winn slipped into her nightgown, sat on the bed with Lucky's front half on her lap, and watched Clay build a fire. *What idea could he possibly have to dispel the mess I've created?* As these troubling thoughts went through her mind, she watched Clay make a few phone calls.

"You won't have to lie. You might have to do some apologizing, though." He explained that there wasn't a single flight available from Montrose or Denver that could get her to Yuma by Christmas. "Just say that you are sorry. That you waited too long to make your new reservation, and you'll let them know as soon as you're able to book a flight."

Clay's idea and the facts held some truth. She needed to make arrangements to get home and wondered why she hadn't thought about that until now. She'd make that call tomorrow. Tonight she needed to fall asleep in Clay's warm, safe arms with their dog at her feet.

Clay tucked her in, pulling the covers up and placing a kiss on her lips. "I'm taking Lucky out for a short walk. We'll be back in a few."

"Okay," she said softly and closed her tired eyes.

Chapter Thirteen

December 24

Winn and Clay met in the dining hall for a quick lunch. Today it was packed with parents and their special needs children. Margie devoted one day every month to an Open Ranch, her version of an Open House. Her guests were looking for a therapeutic environment capable of empowering people of all ages through interaction with horses. Others on the property were horse people who might, someday, give one of the rescued horses a forever home.

Clay barely got a word in. Winn bubbled over with stories of adults and children needing all kinds of help. "The therapy horses are amazing. They're gentle and smart, almost intuitive. They are caregivers, just like me, only a lot more fun."

Her obvious joy and enthusiasm brought a smile to Clay's face. "My morning with the rescue horses was not like that. I can't turn my back on these horses, or they might kick or bite me. The horses you worked with are caregivers. Mine need a whole lot of care. We're at opposite ends in the horse world."

"Yes, but isn't it wonderful that we now share an interest in horses? This experience is opening up a whole new world for me."

He didn't want to burst her bubble, but he knew there weren't many facilities like this one or many paying jobs in this field either. The likelihood of any horse therapy groups existing in Yuma was slim.

"I've got to get back to the arena. Margie is doing a demonstration at 1:15, and I don't want to miss it. See you tonight?" Winn asked.

Clay nodded. *You definitely will.*

He watched her skip away happier than he'd ever seen her. He was confident that his plans for tonight would bring another helping of happiness into her life.

Clay and Winn stood off to the side of the arena, watching Margie address the large group of visitors with her closing comments. The Open Ranch event was over. Some signed up for future therapy sessions, others joined the adoption waiting list.

As the last car drove away, Margie called out, "Hey,

you two. Can you give me a hand putting the therapy horses to bed and giving them each some oats? Randy has plans, and Shellie needs to get home to her kids."

"Sure!" they answered as one voice, thrilled to be working with the horses together.

"And Clay, Braveheart is still out. Take care of him first." Margie went back to her office to finish the day's paperwork, promising to catch up with them in about half an hour.

"Braveheart? Isn't he the horse with so many issues that he was afraid to eat a treat from your hand?"

"That's the one. He's making progress, but he's got a long way to go before he is ready for adoption. I'm surprised Margie is letting me handle him by myself. Keep your distance, okay?"

"Why don't you talk to him the way you talk to dogs and squirrels? There's something very special about your voice. I've seen you in action."

"That's a great idea. I don't think I have talked to him. There were always other people around."

Winn stood back as Clay approached the troubled horse. He was a natural, a horse whisperer, in spite of his limited experience with any equines. He attached a lead rope to the horse's halter and walked him into his stall, speaking softly the entire time. He was so involved, calmly communicating with the horse, that he didn't see Winn climbing up on the interior gate of Braveheart's stall. The horse did and began tossing its head up and down.

"Whoa, there. Easy boy." Braveheart pulled hard on the lead rope. "Hey, Winter, you'd better stand further back. This handsome fellow can be moody. We can't trust him yet."

Winn's foot slipped as she attempted to climb down and she landed on the ground. Clay let go of the horse's lead rope and hurried to help her. Because he was inside the stall, the fast-moving horse reached her first. He poked his muzzle through an opening in the gate, getting as close to her hand as he could and then sniffed.

Winn felt no fear with the gate between them. She was thrilled and elated to be so close to this troubled horse. Sitting up slowly, she offered her open hand to him. First, he nuzzled her empty hand, then he showed his teeth and moved his lips as if he were talking. She laughed, and he did that again. Winn wished she had a carrot or apple to give him.

Clay arrived at her side in mere seconds with a relieved but surprised look on his face. "Winter, how did you get Braveheart to nuzzle the palm of your hand?"

"I didn't do anything special. He just nuzzled me on his own. Nice, huh? His nose is so soft."

"Okay, Miss Horse Charmer, tell your new four-footed boyfriend, adios. We've got the therapy horses to tend to before we can call it a day and enjoy Christmas Eve in our rustic, little cabin."

They headed toward the therapy barn and arena but were stopped by Margie. "You can skip the rest of the horses. Randy was able to get all that done before he left. Have a nice night. Merry Christmas!"

"Good night, Margie," Clay said, tipping his cowboy hat.

"Merry Christmas to you too," added Winn, feeling thankful for having this generous horsewoman in her life. Standing midway between the main house and the therapy barn, she put her arms around Clay and looked lovingly into his eyes. "I'm ready to begin Christmas Eve in our cabin. How about you?"

"Oh, yeah. I'm ready. Let's round up our dog and get this party started."

She wondered if he'd meant her twenty-first birthday party but didn't want to get her hopes up. That was a generic phrase that could mean anything. She couldn't deny they'd had more than a few distractions during their time together.

"Lucky. Come here, Lucky." The dog always came running when either of them called, until tonight. Where was he? He wasn't in the rescue horses' barn, so they checked the therapy horse areas. No luck. No Lucky. They hurried over to the main house and knocked on Margie's front door. Perhaps, he sneaked into the house during the day's event.

"Sorry to bother you. Have you seen Lucky?"

"No. If I see him, I'll bring him to your cabin. Go on home. I'm sure he'll show up."

The sky was dark, and a light snow began to fall. They hurried to the cabin calling for their dog every step of the way. Once there, they'd don their warmest clothes and go back out to look for Lucky.

❄

Clay noticed a faint light coming from the cabin's windows. "I don't remember leaving any lights on. Do you?"

"No. We left at the same time, Lucky, too, and I'm sure there were no lights on then. Maybe one of the guests veered off course, was curious to see one of the cabins, and went in."

Clay's thoughts on the light mystery were more sinister. They had left the cabin door unlocked. Here, they always did. Maybe a thief had gone inside, or Winn's kidnapper had an accomplice. He kept those thoughts to himself, but he picked up a stick the size of a baseball bat in his right hand and put a finger to his lips, signaling for silence as they approached the door.

The cabin's curtains, though revealing the suspicious light, kept them from seeing whatever or whoever might be inside. Opening the door was the only way to know what was going on. Winn held a large rock in one hand and looked ready to use it.

"On the count of three, push open the door and stand back. Ready?"

She nodded, then whispered close to Clay's ear, "With you, I'm ready for anything."

"Okay then. One, two, three!" The door swung

open, and there was Lucky, wearing a red bow around his neck, lying in front of the small woodstove. Elated to find him safe, they knelt beside him, rubbing his ears, patting his head, and hugging his whole body. Standing up, they saw the full effect of what had transpired while they were gone.

Someone had decorated the cabin for Christmas. White lights hung from the entire indoor perimeter, several wreaths decked out the walls, and a tiny tree's multicolored lights sparkled. The table was set with festive placemats, napkins, a bottle of wine, and wine glasses with the outline of a deer etched into each one.

With Lucky sitting at their feet, gazing up with sparkling eyes, and observing their every move, Clay and Winn postponed the kiss that almost happened. They patted his head, scratched his ears, and told him what a good boy he was.

Continuing where they'd left off, Clay kissed her with his eyes before brushing a gentle kiss across her beautiful cream-colored forehead. A slow, dream-worthy kiss followed. Clay could not recall feeling happier than he did at that very moment.

Overcome by an unexpected scent, Clay mumbled, "What's that smell?"

"I don't know, but something smells delicious."

Their eyes looked, their noses sniffed. Sure enough, on the stovetop burners were two pots. One contained ready-to-serve stew, the other resembled some kind of cobbler.

Clay found a card with his name on it under the wine bottle. He opened it and read it silently. The card said, *There is a CD player in the corner by the bed. Press PLAY before you sit down to eat dinner. Your package is wrapped and under the bed. Merry Christmas Eve.*

Following the directions, he went over to the CD player and pressed PLAY. Soft and beautiful holiday music filled the cabin. Winn hummed along as she dished up the stew, and Clay poured the wine.

"I'd like to propose a toast. We faced challenges and survived them all. Winter, we belong together. So, to us, cheers!" He saw dampness forming in her eyes. Tears of joy? He hoped so.

They clinked glasses and took a few sips. Winn scanned the decorated cabin, her eyes finally focusing on Clay's. "I feel as if we're a picture on a Christmas card, so warm and cozy and radiating with love."

Clay lifted her hand and kissed her fingertips. "I have a surprise for you after dinner."

"I have to wait that long?" She laughed.

"Yes, you do. Now, let's eat some of that delicious-smelling stew."

The stew was good, but Clay had other things on his mind and body. To the best of his knowledge, stew was not known to be an aphrodisiac, but tonight might change all that. He took her by the hand and led her to the bed. They sat side-by-side, gazing into each other's eyes. Clay held her face, kissed her temples, her cheeks, and the nape of her neck before running his fingers gently through her long, wavy hair. He guided her tenderly to a lying position, then took a quick look under the bed.

He wasn't quick enough. Winn, propped up on one elbow, with a huge grin on her face, said, "Checking for monsters?"

He squinted his eyes and wiggled his brows. "Yep! And there were none to be found." Clay got up and turned off all the lights except for the tiny white ones, then he pushed all the curtains aside so they could watch the snowflakes drifting down. Lucky was content to lay by the woodstove as it crackled and popped, and the music continued to play.

"Winter, I want to make love with you tonight and every night. I've never felt like this before." He waited for her to say something, anything. Though words did not come, she began to unbutton her blouse. "Let me do that," he said.

They'd slept together before, but far more than sleeping would occur tonight. Clay, as much as he'd like to rip off all of their clothing, took it slow. Each button, each snap brought them closer to the ultimate union. Their breathing, hot and rapid, took a brief detour when Winn worried about *protection*.

"Winter, darling, I promise to make love to you safely, gently, and completely."

"All right, then." She blushed like a sunset on sparkling snow. Wearing only a pair of sexy red panties and matching bra, she watched Clay stand and remove all of his clothing. His desire for her was obvious.

He joined her under the covers, loving her scent and the feel of her skin. Being near her raised his body heat to a degree he'd never thought possible. At the same time, she brought out the goodness in him, the tenderness he didn't know he possessed.

When his hand cupped her breast, a faint whimper escaped her lips. When that hand journeyed lower, she froze briefly. His touch had taken her breath away.

"Would you like me to stop?"

"No, but please be patient. I feel like I'm losing control."

"I think that's a good thing," he said, tickling her bottom lip with his finger. "Relax, darling. I love you, and I'll never hurt you." He moved his hand slowly up the inside of her thigh and then to her sweet spot. Her breathing quickened at his touch.

Winn slid her arms around his neck and surrendered to his caresses. Her moans encouraged him to head for the finish line, the ultimate sensation. *Joy to the world.* He loved Winter more than life itself. He entered slowly, gently, watching her beautiful face for the slightest sign of distress. She arched her back and raised her hips to meet him. Pure joy was what he saw. They held each other tightly until their naked bodies moved rhythmically as one, exploding together in a flurry of flashing, swirling white light, as if in a snow globe that had been shaken.

As they lay together, regaining their strength and beginning to breathe normally, Lucky jumped onto the bed, wanting attention. They put their clothes back on, knowing they'd take Lucky for a walk in the snow before the evening was over.

"Cobbler time," Winn announced.

"And, birthday present time," he said with a wink and a smile.

"I thought you just gave me my birthday present."

"There's more." He pulled the present out from under the bed. It was wrapped with gold paper and topped with a large red bow. "Come on, Winter. Open it."

"You remembered." Her face held a mixture of happy and sad.

"Yes, ma'am. It's your twenty-first Christmas Eve birthday. A very special day, indeed."

"My family never did much about birthdays, so this is extra special for me. Thank you, Clay."

"Don't thank me until you open it."

She stared at the beautiful package. She tried to shake it, but it was too large. When she opened the top of the box, she laughed. "This is a trick, huh?" Inside the big box was a card and twenty small boxes surrounded by white packing peanuts. "Which one should I open first?"

Clay shrugged. "The order doesn't matter."

The contents of the first box produced a delighted squeal from Winn's mouth. It contained a snow globe with two horses inside. She shook it immediately to make the snow dance around the animals. Next, she threw her arms around Clay. "This is the best birthday ever. You've managed to know me so well in such a short time. How can I ever thank you?"

"For starters, you could open the card and the rest of the boxes." He was curious about the card because he had not placed a card in the box. Maybe he should have opened it first.

She nodded, opened the card, and handed it to Clay. He read it out loud. "Come for Christmas breakfast at the main house tomorrow morning. I know something you don't know." It was signed by Margie." Winn looked at Clay and shrugged. He gave her an I-don't-know-either look back. They both agreed that breakfast would be nice and wondered what Margie knew.

Winn returned to the joyful, present-opening task. Each box held a snow globe; each snow globe contained a different scene. There were twenty in all. Winn jumped up, went over to the side of the bed, and began rummaging through the duffle bag holding her clothes. "I found it!"

Clay watched, wondering what she was up to. He could tell she was delighted, and that was all that mattered. She came back with another snow globe in her hand. It was the first one he had given her on the last day of her fantasy vacation. She set it with the others. Clay's gift of twenty-one snow globes brought tears to her eyes.

"Are you sad, Winter?"

"No. I'm happy." *Maybe, too happy.*

Winn, Lucky, and Clay sat on the braided rug, their bodies warmed by the woodstove, their ears soothed by the music, and their eyes delighted by twinkling lights. Together, in love, on a cold winter's night.

Chapter Fourteen

December 25

No specific time had been stated on the breakfast invitation, so they waited until nine to arrive, thinking that was a reasonable hour for a Christmas breakfast. Clay knocked on the door using the horseshoe-shaped metal knocker. When no answer came, he knocked harder. Still, no one came to the door.

Winn cracked it open and heard music. "Hello? Margie? We're here for breakfast." Odd. There was still no reply. "Clay, there could be a problem. We'd better go in."

All the interior holiday lights were on, music played, and the scent of cinnamon rolls and oranges filled the air. They walked curiously through the living area taking notice of the crackling fire in the huge stone fireplace. Next, they entered the dining room, where the large table was set for two. They checked the kitchen, hoping to find Margie or someone.

No Margie, but there was a note. Winn handed it to Clay. He read, "I've been called away for a few hours. Make yourselves at home. The hot portion of your breakfast is in the oven, the chilled part, in the fridge. I'm confident you'll figure it out. Enjoy!" Clay looked surprised. "I suppose that means we won't find out what she knows that we don't know." He chuckled, sure the woman was toying with them.

"I'll dish up our breakfast. Why don't you go back and get Lucky. We should all be together. I'm sure Margie wouldn't mind."

"Back in a flash!"

Winn sang along with the Christmas carols as she brought the food out to the table. She took the clinging wrap from the bowl of cold fruit and poured orange juice into the glasses. She was removing the foil from the hot plates when Clay and Lucky returned, each wearing a smile.

"And what, besides this delicious-smelling meal, is the reason for your extreme exuberance?" Winn asked.

Clay held out his arms and made a 360-degree turn. "This, all of this, everything. You, Lucky, our time at the ranch. I got my fantasy and so much more."

They sat down and began eating. "I feel the same

way you do. Though my fantasy vacation got off to a bad start, and we had our share of difficulties, I wouldn't trade a minute of it. Everything that happened brought us closer together. I feel like I've been living a fairytale." She sighed as a feeling of melancholy washed over her. "I just wish it didn't have to end."

Lucky barked and ran to the front door. He'd heard something. Snow sliding off the metal roof? A coyote? A horse that escaped from the barn? The door opened.

"Oh, good. You're still here." Margie was back, a manila envelope in her hand. "I'm sorry I wasn't here to greet you."

"Do you want something to eat? There's plenty left," asked Winn.

"No thanks. I ate hours ago. But I'll take some coffee."

Winn dashed into the kitchen to retrieve a cup. She was shocked when Margie added a shot of whiskey to her cup-a-joe.

"You might want a shot of this too. There is something I must tell you. I have a brother who lives in Montana on a ranch ten times the size of this one. He needs my help."

Margie explained these new circumstances, though vaguely. She stalled, hesitating to share whatever it was she needed to tell them. "Long story short. I've sold the ranch. As of this morning, it's a done deal."

Clay frowned. "Do we need to leave right away?"

"It's more complicated than that," Margie said, beginning to pace with the envelope rolled up in her hand.

Clay and Winn shared disappointed, desperate looks. Their fabulous time together was screeching to a sudden halt.

Margie handed one page from the packet of papers for Clay and Winn to look at. Winn looked, Clay read, but its contents made no sense. The legal-looking paper was a Quitclaim Deed naming Clay Washington and Winter Wahlberg the new owners of the ranch.

"No, this is impossible." Winn felt dizzy. "We love this ranch, but we can't afford to buy anything at this point in our lives."

"She's right, Margie. Wait. There's got to be a catch. What's the catch?"

"No catch. I've needed to sell the ranch for a while but had no offers until that guy, Martin, showed up. He made it all happen. Said he worked for The Fantasy Maker. Weird, huh? I was leery, of course, until he offered cash. It's a win-win for us all." Margie stood up and left, saying she had lots to do.

Alone again, Winn couldn't believe what had occurred. "Pinch me, Clay. Prove to me that I'm not dreaming and this is real. This sounds too good to be true, and we both know what they say about that."

Instead of pinching her, he kissed her with so much warmth and passion that she knew their latest miracle had to be real. He picked her up and, holding her close, spun her around. Winning the lottery could not have been any better. Dreams do come true! Looking at each other, they spoke the same words at the same time. "We'd better make some calls."

Winn wasn't ready to talk to anyone. "You go first. I haven't decided what to say."

Sitting together on the large sofa in front of the fireplace, Clay took out his cell phone. "Hi Dad, Hi Mom. You'd better sit down. I have some news." His call was short, to the point, supplying the few known details. "Your turn." He handed her his cell phone and pulled her onto his lap.

"Merry Christmas, Mom. I have so much to tell you and Dad."

Mrs. Wahlberg began her questioning, and she didn't sound happy. Winn tapped the speaker button, so Clay could hear. "Start talking, young lady. You've been gone nearly two weeks. Did you learn a lot? Do you think you'll get that promotion?" Her questions were non-stop. Questions Winn had no intention of answering right now. "When will you be home?"

Clay put both arms around her for support. Feeling so much love in her heart, not even her upset mother could spoil her happiness on this miraculous Christmas morning. She smiled at Clay before replying.

"We'll visit soon, I promise. Don't worry. I'm fine. Dad, hang on to your hat. I am now the co-owner of a horse therapy ranch in Colorado." She hoped that once her parents understood her good fortune, her new life, and her new love, they'd be happy for her. "And Mom, I've met that cool drink of water," Winn couldn't help giggling, "and I'm incredibly thirsty."

A NOTE FROM THE AUTHOR

Thank you for reading Winter's Blush. I hope you enjoyed reading the story as much as I enjoyed writing it. When writing, I often play music that fits the scene, the mood, or the season. In this case, my music selections consisted of various instrumental Christmas tunes. Yes—no vocals. I find that distracting, and I tend to sing along. I also listened to Vivaldi's "Presto" when writing the tense or dangerous scenes and Ian Post's "I Must be Dreaming" during the sweet loving scenes. I have to admit it is the mood music that gets me started, but sometimes, when my brain begins to spin with words coming faster than I can type, the music ends, and I don't even notice.

If you've read any of my other books, you know that I find a way to include a wonderful dog in each and every story. Lucky, this book's dog, was inspired by a real dog with the same name. He, too, was a rescue and now splits his time between Southern Arizona and the Colorado mountains.

We still don't know who The Fantasy Maker really is, but I wish he or she or?? would make my fantasy come true: Turn one of my books into a TV series or movie. In the meantime, I'll keep writing. Eventually, a book titled: The Fantasy Maker Revealed or The Reunion will close out this series. So, stay tuned. I always include new book releases, special prices, and news about my adventures or misadventures in my monthly newsletter. You're invited to check it out and subscribe at the link below.

https://www.cricketrohman.org.

Keep scrolling for a couple of Winn's recipes.

TEA AND NOODLES
Mountain Recipes by Winn

Mountain Cranberry Tea

5-8 cranberries per cup
a dash of honey
a splash of flavored brandy (optional)
Winn likes peach flavored brandy
Of course, if you wish to have a more traditional tea
flavor, drop in a tea bag.

- Place cranberries in cup or mug.
- Pour boiling water over berries and let them soak for a minute.
- Using a fork, poke, then smash berries against the side of the cup.
- Add a few drops of honey.
- Add a splash of flavored brandy. (optional- Winn likes peach.)
- Steep for stronger flavor.

Winn's Mountain Noodles

1 cup of water
A package of ramen noodles
½ tbsp of olive oil
1 tsp of Italian seasoning – or equal parts of basil, garlic, oregano, thyme
¼ cup of pine nuts
A sprinkle of grated cheese (Winn likes Romano, but any will do.)
Salt and pepper (optional)

- Boil water and add noodles (Winn does NOT use the flavor pack often included with the noodles but you can.)
- Add oil.
- Cook and stir with a fork until soft.
- Add Italian seasoning. Stir.
- Add pine nuts. Stir.
- Remove from heat and sprinkle with cheese.

The noodle recipe is perfect for lunch for one or a snack for two.

Simply, double the recipe for lunch for two.

And, feel free to modify to your tastes.

ENJOY!

What's Next?

**More standalone stories in
The Fantasy Maker Series.**

SUMMER'S ISLAND

JD won a contest and ended up on a deserted island
somewhere in Micronesia.
This is a wild beach adventure complete with danger,
love, and a dog named Noodles.

AUTUMN'S GHOST

When Ranger learns of his odd inheritance, he enlists
Autumn's help to create a haunted house. October in
New Hampshire is gorgeous, fun and games for sure,
but evil lurks.

Goodreads

BookBub

Thank You!

Thank you for reading *Winter's Blush.*
Would you like to know when Cricket's next book is available? That's easy. Sign up for Cricket's (almost) monthly NEWSLETTER and you'll receive notifications of new books, giveaways, and other exclusive content. https://www.cricketrohman.org

If you enjoyed this story, please leave a REVIEW on Goodreads, Bookbub, or your favorite online retailer.

Reviews are helpful to readers and appreciated by authors.

About the Author

Cricket Rohman grew up in Estes Park, Colorado and spent her formative years among deer, coyotes, and fields of beautiful blue columbine. After retiring from a career in education, she became a full-time author writing contemporary fiction and western series and sagas about teachers, cowboys, dogs, lovers, and creative women inventing unique careers—just to mention a few.

**Cricket loves to hear from readers.
Connect with her via:**

Website https://www.cricketrohman.org

Facebook https://facebook.com/CricketRohmanAuthor

Twitter https://twitter.com/CricketRohman

Bookbub https://www.bookbub.com/authors/cricket-rohman

www.goodreads.com/author/show/112683.
Cricket_Rohman

Email cricketrohman@gmail.com

MORE BOOKS BY CRICKET ROHMAN

You will find the links and excerpts for all of Cricket Rohman's books
https://www.cricketrohman.org

❄

The Fantasy Maker Series
Contemporary Adventures

SUMMER'S ISLAND
JD won a contest and ended up on a deserted island somewhere in Micronesia.
This is a wild beach adventure complete with danger, love, and a dog named Noodles.

AUTUMN'S GHOST
When Ranger learns of his odd inheritance, he enlists Autumn's help to create a haunted house. October in New Hampshire is gorgeous, fun and games for sure, but evil lurks.

WINTER'S BLUSH
The Fantasy Maker strikes an agreement with Clay. What's the catch? He must pretend to be someone he's not. A quick read that includes mountain hiking, rescue dogs, danger, and yes, some romance.

The McAllister Brothers Series
Romantic Western Adventures

COLORADO TAKEDOWN Book 1
This twisty cowboy adventure includes treachery
new love, family, courage, and amazing ranch animals.

MONTANA COUNTDOWN Book 2
A wealthy rancher's story-telling tendency entices two
eavesdroppers—a greedy criminal and a would-be
novelist—to venture to his Montana ranch to search for
his hidden treasure.

WYOMING SUNDOWN Book 3
Clint McAllister's challenge put his sons in grave
danger. Alice is furious about his foolish plan.
It was almost Christmas, a bad time for such nonsense.

WILD WEDDINGS Book 4
Family, fate, and formidable danger make loving and
laughing a challenge.
Trace and Troy love two city gals. Their love is strong
but their plan for new ranches and happy lives is
threatened at every turn. Who wishes them harm?

The Creative Hearts Sweet Romance Series
Creative Women Standalone Novellas

PHOEBE'S PHOTO FETISH

Phoebe Foxglove had three loves: Photography, Flowers, and Bobby.
Two out of the three served her well.

TINA'S TASTY TOURS
Tina has an impossible dream that comes with a substantial price tag. In the meantime, she works at the Punk Patio and a 1960s diner where she is required to look like Marilyn Monroe.

CAITLIN'S COW WASH
Caitlin feels trapped and out of place living in an old-fashion Leave It To Beaver household. Then, a perfect, win-win solution comes along—a cowboy named Cooper.

ANNA'S ANIMAL HOUSE
Desert gal ends up with a Pacific Northwest ranch where animals flock to her. She's a fish out of water but learns to cope, even thrive, in spite of an ongoing feud with the handsome veterinarian.

The Lindsey Lark Series
Fiction with Elements of Romance & Mystery

WANTED: AN HONEST MAN Book 1
Lindsey, a kinder teacher in survival mode after an unthinkable divorce, is brilliant in the classroom. Unfortunately, unwanted sinister challenges invade her

off-hours.

LETTERS, LOVERS, & LIES Book 2
Jake and Lindsey are in love, but so much stands in
their way.
Fortunately, they are smart, multi-talented, and they
love to laugh. Wendell, the 180-pound lovable mastiff, is
featured throughout this series.

HIT THE ROAD, JAKE! Book 3
Thrilling, romantic, and sprinkled with humor, this
novel reinvents the 'buddy movie' concept with the
written word... and a pretty woman. As Jake and
Lindsey travel from Tucson to Estes Park in their RV,
the dangers they face become deadly.

Saving Madeline
Standalone Contemporary Fiction
An entertaining story with humor, emotion,
and an unusual mother-daughter relationship.
Audiobook available too.

Christmas in the North Woods
A Children's Picture Book
Oliver Owl introduces the reader to his forest friends
who are busy rehearsing for the annual Christmas Song
Contest.
Audiobook available too.